LIES WITHIN THE DARKEST TOWER

DESPERATE DISGUISE BOOK 1

TESSA COLE

Gryphon's Gate Publishing

Gryphon's Gate Publishing
550 King St. N.
PO Box 42088 Conestoga
Waterloo, ON
N2L 6K5

Print ISBN: 978-1-990587-61-0

CHAPTER 1
Sage

"BRING YOUR GUARD UP. YOUR GUARD!" the armsmaster of Herstind Castle yelled, his sharp words carrying from the far side of the bailey all the way to the step outside the kitchen door where I sat.

My pulse jumped. Yelling like that could only mean one thing: the armsmaster was training my younger brother in the middle of the day's sweltering heat.

I dropped the potato I'd been scrubbing back into the bucket and jerked to my feet, but Udara, the Herstind Keep cook who sat beside me also scrubbing vegetables, grabbed my wrist, stopping me.

"It's your stepfather's command," she said, shading eyes too wide with fear against the glaring sun and glancing up at the hazy summer sky. "No one would train in this heat if they were given a choice. Pylos isn't a fool."

She was right. The Herstind Keep armsmaster was a gruff man, as rough and cruel as my stepfather, but not a fool. And neither was my stepfather.

"He isn't even trying to hide his intentions anymore." I yanked my wrist free, grabbed a fist-full of skirt in each hand to avoid tripping, and raced around the keep, praying that this time wouldn't be the time where Sawyer's body gave out on him.

He was all I had left and as much as I wanted to run away from our stepfather's rule, I wasn't going to leave him behind.

Except if things kept going the way they were, if our stepfather, Lord Edred Wyare, Marquis of Herstind March, got his way, Sawyer would die just like our parents and other brother had.

His sword training, or rather his *beatings* since there was no way he'd ever have the stamina to become a good swordsman, had been coming more and more frequently, giving him less time to recover between lessons.

And while our stepfather told his soldiers — who were no better than the brigands we defended the March from — that he was making a man of Sawyer, everyone, including the soldiers, knew Edred was really hoping the lessons would kill him. He was, after all, Edred's heir, a point of shame Edred constantly reminded Sawyer of.

And things had only gotten worse this spring when Edred married his new wife. She could give him an heir of his own blood, and while she wasn't pregnant yet, she was young enough — younger than me by a few years even — and Edred must have felt confident she soon would be and wasn't going to keep Sawyer around.

Especially since Sawyer would turn sixteen next season and be able to petition the king to get our father's land back. The land Edred only controlled because he'd married our mother. Edred wasn't the marquis by birth and Sawyer was, and that meant Edred's time of running the March into poverty was almost at an end.

If Sawyer survived.

Which was why Edred was doing everything in his power to ensure Sawyer had an unfortunate accident. He couldn't just kill Sawyer. That would draw suspicion from the throne and the king could send inquisitors to look into the matter.

And while I loved my brother dearly and knew he wasn't an idiot, he was a complete fool when it came to our family's land.

He should just run away. We wouldn't have much — there wasn't much left in the keep we could take and sell — but we'd at least be away from Edred.

But Sawyer wasn't going to allow Edred to continue ruling our people through fear, and he wasn't going to let the brigands hiding in the wastelands at the edge of our border continue growing in number. Herstind was already poor, the wild, rugged land hard to farm, and Edred had pretty much pillaged his own people to provide himself with the lavish lifestyle he'd adopted the moment our mother had died eight years ago.

"It won't stop until you bring up your guard," Pylos yelled. "Defend yourself."

My pulse pounded faster. If Pylos was telling Sawyer to defend himself that meant the man was likely whacking away at him, as if that would somehow make Sawyer regain his bearings and his breath and figure out how to fight back.

Which was ridiculous. Yes, fighters needed to be pushed past their limit to grow, but Sawyer could trip over his own feet without moving. Beating him relentlessly and expecting him to fight back wasn't going to work. He just wasn't at that skill level and I doubted he ever would be.

I rounded the corner and stumbled.

It wasn't Pylos fighting Sawyer. He stood to the side, leaning against the stable wall, his arms crossed, his weathered, deeply tanned face twisted with a satisfied sneer, watching as our stepfather whacked the flat of his blade against the side of Sawyer's unprotected head.

My brother staggered and fell to one knee, and it was clear, even though they were on the far side of the bailey near the stables, he was fighting to breathe.

"Get up," Edred snarled, his big, burly form towering over Sawyer.

Despite the fact Edred was training, he wore his regular clothes, a loose-fitting cotton shirt with the sleeves rolled up and half the buttons undone, revealing the thick scars crisscrossing his large chest. He usually had at least two days worth of scruff on his chin, cheeks, and scalp, but today his skin was smooth — likely because he'd known he'd be training during the day's hottest hours.

As usual, he fought with his regular heavy two-handed sword, the blade always sharp and ready and not a blunt practice weapon, partly because he didn't care if he hurt Sawyer and partly because with Sawyer's meager skill level, he'd have no problem controlling the fight and doubted he'd accidentally kill him.

It was the 'didn't care if he hurt him' part that made me furious, and I knew the only reason our mother had married Edred was because she'd needed a husband to rule the March, and he'd been a general for the King's army and had the strongest political connections as well as martial and tactical training.

That and His Majesty had pushed for Edred. And while our mother had lived, he'd been fine... or maybe

I'd just been too young and naive to have noticed the truth about him.

Sawyer, on the other hand, was his opposite in every way, his frame slight, his features, like mine, sharp. On me they called it refined, if a little too severe to be beautiful. On him they called it overly feminine — which was another reason Edred found Sawyer wanting as a man.

At a quick glance strangers assumed we were twins even though he was five years younger than me. We had the same small build and brown eyes that, depending on the light, were flecked with green, the same red hair more commonly seen on northerners, and the same pale skin that burned in a heartbeat if we weren't careful. All of which we'd gotten from our mother. Unlike Edred, Sawyer was weighed down with a heavily padded practice tunic that was supposed to protect him, but really meant that Pylos, or in this case Edred, could hit him harder without fear of breaking skin.

"Get up," Edred barked.

Sawyer coughed and gasped and struggled to stand, but Edred didn't wait. He smashed his blade against Sawyer's back, toppling him forward and drawing a strangled, phlegmy cry.

"You're making this too easy." He whacked Sawyer again and again, not giving him the chance to get up, and I knew from having faced the brunt of Edred's cruel nature that Sawyer's world was reeling. I couldn't imagine all that on top of not being able to breathe.

Another whack and Sawyer dropped his sword, curled in on himself, and covered his head.

"Get. Up," Edred snarled, his ruddy face even redder with the heat.

Great Father above, I had to stop this. Edred took pleasure in suffering, and while I'd thought he wouldn't outright kill Sawyer, watching him hit my brother again and again as his expression brightened with wicked glee made me doubt my initial assumption.

Maybe this was the day Edred wouldn't care what the king thought. Maybe he'd figured out how to dispose of Sawyer's body and not raise suspicion... which meant he'd have figured out how to dispose of me as well, since he knew I'd go to the king myself to beg for justice if Sawyer went missing. It wouldn't matter that I was just a woman. I'd create so much trouble, be so loud and disobedient that someone would have to listen to me.

"Useless child," he spat, raising his blade and turning his wrist so he'd strike with the sharpened edge.

"No." I bolted toward them. I didn't have time to beg as expected of me, and I doubted Edred would even notice me if I acted like I was supposed to.

CHAPTER 2
Sage

I BARRELED INTO EDRED, rammed my shoulder into his chest — which didn't even make him stumble — and shoved my forearm up against his biceps to stop his downward swing, just like the previous armsmaster had taught Sawyer and me.

It was a foolish move for far too many reasons. I was a lady. I was supposed to be demure, barely seen and not at all heard. I certainly wasn't supposed to touch a man without being told to and I was never supposed to throw myself into the middle of a fight. I'd also been warned that even though I was stronger than the average woman of my build and station — thanks to the servants' duties forced on me — I didn't stand a chance grappling with someone like Edred who was significantly stronger, taller, and heavier than me.

If I was going to defy what was expected of me and

fight him, my best strategy would be quick strikes, never letting him get his hands on me. Better yet, from a distance with a bow.

Of course, if I had a bow and I didn't care about consequences, Edred would already be dead.

But I didn't have a bow, let alone a sword, and stopping his strike while his hand was still up in the air and before he could put his full strength behind his swing was my only option.

"Out of my way, girl." He pushed me aside and I hit the ground with a heavy *umph,* rolled back onto my feet, and flung myself back at Edred as he swung at Sawyer's back.

My shoulder hit him low in the gut, drawing a grunt. He shoved me back, and I lost my balance and landed on my butt on the hardpacked dirt beside Sawyer.

Edred's eyes narrowed.

"Looks like someone needs a lesson in obedience," Pylos drawled, still leaning against the rough-hewn stable wall.

"Looks like," Edred said, his voice low, freezing the churning fear in my stomach for Sawyer into terror for myself.

I'd thought my safety had been just as guaranteed as Sawyer's. I was a nobleman's daughter and even if I wasn't considered beautiful, I was still a political prize which meant I'd fetch a high bride price. And the only reason Edred hadn't married me off yet — or rather married me off *again* — was because he was still waiting for the king to declare my betrothed dead. Something I prayed wouldn't happen for at least another season, hopefully more since Sawyer might have to wait months to have his petition heard by the king.

"Pick it up," Edred said, glaring at me.

"What?"

Edred jerked his chin at Sawyer's blunt practice sword. "Pick it up."

"I—" Sure, I knew how to fight. I'd been learning alongside Sawyer since I was ten. I'd been fascinated with the skill and had begged the previous armsmaster to teach me when he started teaching Sawyer. For some reason — with my mother's blessing — he'd defied societal expectations and taught me. But Edred had replaced that armsmaster and the last four years hadn't been learning as much as trying to help Sawyer improve in secret to save him from Pylos's beatings.

Even if I'd been steadily growing as a swordsman, I doubted I was anywhere near Edred's caliber. He was a hardened soldier. Not to mention Sawyer's sword wasn't sharp, and while I might be able to score a touch against Edred, I wouldn't be able to hurt him — even if I used the weapon like a club — and that would only infuriate him.

"Pick. It. Up," Edred snarled.

"Sage, don't," Sawyer gasped, reaching for his weapon, his breaths short and shallow and wet.

The darkness of a premonition fluttered across my vision and a sudden crushing fear swept through me overwhelming all other fears. I didn't have to try to figure out what my strange premonition was trying to tell me this time. I knew without a doubt if Sawyer picked up his sword, Edred would kill him.

I snatched the weapon and stood, praying that Edred also wasn't planning to kill me, too.

A dangerous glint darkened Edred's eyes and I yanked my attention to my feet, hoping an act of submission would end this.

"That's it, girl," Edred snarled. "Now come at me."

My gaze leaped back up to him as my pulse roared in my ears and my hands shook, making the practice blade tremble. Edred wasn't even in a fighting stance and his sword was lowered, but I wasn't foolish enough to think I could catch him off guard.

For a moment, I considered actually trying to fight him, showing him and everyone else that I wasn't helpless, that I didn't need them or anyone else to protect me — not that they'd been protecting me. Being protected by the men in your life was just a fantasy, something girls told themselves because their fathers and brothers had complete control of their lives.

But I couldn't win against Edred, and it would be foolish to reveal just how much training I'd received. It was bad enough I'd blocked Edred to protect Sawyer, defying how I was supposed to behave. No, I needed to look weak, not draw Edred's suspicion, and wait for the right moment. Being able to surprise him or one of his men might be the advantage Sawyer and I needed during an escape. At the very least, I needed to wait until I had a weapon that could actually hurt him.

"Come at me!" he roared, making me jump.

I rushed at him, swinging the heavy practice blade in a wide, sloppy arc toward Edred's side. The arms-master who'd taught me would have cringed at the attack, but I had to do something. I couldn't just stand there and cower even if that was what was expected of me. Disobeying Edred would only make him angrier.

He blocked my attack with a vicious, one-handed stroke that wrenched my blade down and swung a back-handed strike at my head.

Instinct kicked in and I carried through with my already forward and down movement, ducking his strike. I scrambled out of the way instead of swinging at his calves like I'd been taught and rolled to my feet.

With a growl, Edred lunged, barely giving me a chance to bring my sword up. He swung at my shoulder. The strike was obvious, and while it was still fast, it was slower than his usual strikes.

I scrambled back, yanking my sword up to block. The impact jarred through my hands and up my arms, and I gritted my teeth and hung on. Except I wasn't supposed to hang on. I was supposed to be a weak, unskilled swordsman, and if Sawyer and I were going to get through this, I needed to just take Edred's punishment and pray hurting me was enough to satiate his need for violence and he wouldn't turn his attention back to Sawyer.

He swung again, another wide, obvious strike to my shoulder, and I brought my sword up again, holding it out too far like a novice. Our blades collided and this time I couldn't soften the impact with my arms and keep my grip.

The strike knocked the sword from my hands, sending it flying, and Edred lunged in at full speed. His blade skimmed dangerously close to my ribs, and before I could jerk out of the way, he grabbed the front of my dress. With a snarl, he shoved me to the ground, and kicked me in the stomach.

My breath exploded from my lungs.

"Get up." He kicked me again, the impact screaming through my chest. "Come on. Get up."

I fought to catch my breath, but he kicked a third time, then grabbed a handful of my long hair and jerked me up. "Will you interfere in a lesson again?"

"No, my lord," I gasped.

He smashed the back of his hand against my face. Pain exploded in my cheek and the metallic tang of blood seeped over my tongue. The world spun around me and a far-off distant part of me realized he'd split my lip.

"I'd hoped you'd have learned by now."

Except I was pretty sure he hoped I'd never learn.

He hit me again, letting me fall back to the ground. Dark specks danced across my vision and my ears rang, and he drew his foot back for another kick but stopped.

"What?" he snarled, picking up his sword where he'd dropped it and turning toward someone just out of sight.

"A fae," Udara's youngest son said. "Dressed in black. Coming up the road."

"About time," Edred replied. "Looks like the lottery has finally come to Herstind Keep."

A new dread filled me. I didn't need a premonition to know it wouldn't be any of Edred's men forced to make the sacrifice. It would be Sawyer.

CHAPTER 3
Sage

"Should I gather the men?" Pylos asked, pushing away from the wall, his gaze flickering to Sawyer before returning to Edred.

I wasn't sure from that look if he knew what was going on or not, but given the timing, it was obvious Edred had somehow arranged for Sawyer's name to be drawn in the lottery even though he was still a season too young and the heir to Herstind March.

It was the perfect way to get rid of him. The summons would force Sawyer to go to the Black Tower by tomorrow or the next day at the latest, and the magic binding him to the Tower wouldn't allow him to return unless he was given special permission.

It didn't matter that his name shouldn't have been in the lottery. I had no doubt Edred was betting on the rigors of training and defending the Gates of the

Realms on killing him before anyone realized the truth. Sawyer could even claim he shouldn't have been called, but anyone looking for dispensation had to have his lord petition the king on his behalf, and Edred was Sawyer's lord. Given that I was sure this was Edred's doing, I doubted he'd agree to Sawyer's petition.

"Only gather those young enough to make the sacrifice," Edred said, carrying out the pretense that he didn't really know whose name was going to be on the summons. But his lips curled back in a wicked grin, his pleasure and the truth obvious.

Pylos gave a curt nod and hurried toward the keep to summon everyone not patrolling the area who was between sixteen and twenty-six years old to gather in the great hall.

Edred kicked me again, the half-hearted thump making my already bruised chest ache and stealing my breath for a moment but thankfully not adding to my injuries.

"Get up, girl, and greet our guest. And you—" He turned his almost gleeful expression to Sawyer. "Hurry and clean up. You're Herstind's heir. Don't embarrass me in front of a fae lord."

"Yes, my lord," Sawyer gasped as he staggered to his feet, his breath wheezing, each inhalation strained and wet.

Edred strode toward the keep and Sawyer held out

his hand to help me up, but his breath rattled in his chest and a coughing fit bent him over.

"Are you... all right?" he forced out between gasping breaths.

He looked afraid, but not with the fear of being forced to leave everything never to return. It was the fear that Edred could have finally snapped and killed both of us. He hadn't figured out that he was the sacrifice or if he had, he thought there was a way around it.

And maybe there was. Maybe he could survive long enough in the Gray to convince someone to let him petition the king without going through Edred.

"I said clean up," Edred barked from halfway across the bailey, making Sawyer flinch.

"Go." I jerked my chin after Edred, urging him to follow.

If, for some reason, Sawyer's name wasn't on the summons, then it would be bad if he wasn't presentable in front of the fae.

Even if the fae was a member of the Black Guard, he was still a fae, and fae were far more powerful than humans. Not only were they stronger and faster, and potentially had centuries worth of experience because they lived longer than humans, they had magic. And while it was possible for humans to possess magic — and more powerful magic than fae — a human sorcerer hadn't been seen in almost two hundred years. That, and even if it was just a little bit, every fae possessed some kind of magic, and no one wanted to risk upsetting a fae just in case his little-bit-of-magic was deadly.

I rolled to my hands and knees so I could sit up, my chest and left side throbbing in protest. It wasn't the worst beating Edred had given me, but I was still going to be sore and black and blue for days.

Udara's boy, Dodd, stared at me with enormous brown eyes. His small body trembled, and I didn't know if it was fear from having interrupted Edred or fear over the way of our world.

Every boy, unless he was a nobleman's heir or unable to wield a weapon, spent ten years in the lottery.

That was the deal we'd made with the fae five hundred years ago after the Shadow Gate had opened, and a great evil had threatened both of our realms.

The fae and the Five Great Kingdoms of Man had banded together to push back the monsters that had rushed out, and after many horrible battles, the Shadow Gate had been sealed and the three towers had been formed. The White Tower in the fae realm, a place of knowledge and learning for human and fae scholars, the Gold Tower in the human realm, where humans and fae gather to discuss political issues among their kingdoms, and the Black Tower in the Gray, the first line of defense if the Shadow Gate ever opened again.

And while the gate had been sealed for centuries, that didn't mean life in the Black Guard was easy. They were a force that needed to be ready at a moments notice and were constantly training. As well, the Gray, where the Tower stood between the Three Gates of the Realms, still had monsters lurking in its mists, remnants of the creatures who'd poured through the Shadow Gate all those years ago.

Those called to make the sacrifice had to leave everything behind, even if they were already married and had children, and they were bound by magic that wouldn't let them run away from their duty. Which made a part of me furious.

I understood we needed to maintain an army in the Gray, but my father had died shortly after Sawyer had been born, my other brother — between me and Sawyer — had died from the sweating sickness a few winters after that, and my mother died just over eight summers ago. I knew what it felt like to lose someone, knew how hard it was to overcome that loss, and didn't want anyone to suffer that. But then, if marriage and children got you out of the lottery, men would rush to marry, and all the newest Black Guard sacrifices would be boys barely past their sixteenth birthday.

I stood and tried to dust myself off, but with sweat dampening my clothes and slicking my face and forearms, I only managed to smear it. My hand brushed the pendant my mother had given me for my twelfth birthday and my throat tightened with the grief I always felt when I thought of her. It wasn't the sobbing heartache it had been when she'd first died, but there was still an ache that I didn't think would ever go away.

I resisted the urge to pull it out from under my bodice and check on it. For some reason, Edred had forgotten about it, and I wasn't going to draw his or anyone else's attention to it. The pendant was small, but it was still an emerald wrapped in gold filigree. I kept it on a string so it didn't look like I was wearing anything of value, because if he thought it was valuable, he'd take it and sell it, just like he'd sold the rest of Mother's jewelry and everything else that had belonged to her.

My heart ached. I missed her so much. I missed her warm smile and bright laughter, and I missed climbing into bed with her and Sawyer and listening to her read adventure tales to us until we fell asleep. She wouldn't have wanted Sawyer to have suffered Edred's temper just to keep our family's land. Of course, she would have also understood Sawyer staying to keep his claim on the land so he could take it back.

And now all that suffering had been for nothing, because even if I stayed, I wouldn't be able to hold his claim on Herstind March. Edred would most likely kill me — inquisitors weren't sent for women who died mysteriously — or he'd push the king to pronounce my betrothed dead and marry me to someone else.

No, if Sawyer was leaving, so was I. I wasn't going to stay, and while I'd dreamed of travelling to the far south and becoming a Sayorian Swordmaiden — because they were real, they had to be — that plan could wait until I'd figured out how to free Sawyer from the Black Guard.

"Come on," I said to Dodd, jerking my chin toward the gatehouse.

Dodd continued to stare at me and tremble.

"The fae lord isn't here for you," I said, smoothing a hand over my hair in an attempt to look more presentable.

If I really cared, I'd find a mirror, but this fae lord wasn't a potential husband Edred could sell me to, so he didn't care if I looked like a nobleman's daughter or not. I wasn't his daughter, so I didn't matter. "You don't even have to speak to him, just tend to his horse."

I held out my hand and he took it and we walked to the gatehouse.

The guard on duty was one of Edred's staunch supporters who'd come with him from the King's army to join the Herstind forces. Sawyer's lesson had been out in the open and close enough to the gate that the guard had to have seen Edred kicking me, but the man just gave me a dry look and turned his attention back to the road.

Of course, I didn't expect much from him or anyone in the castle. There were only a few men left from when my mother had been alive, and they kept quiet for the sake of their families. Everyone else was loyal to Edred and while he'd made it clear no one was to touch me or Sawyer without permission, he'd also made it clear, no one was to help us, either.

A few seconds later I heard the thud of hooves on the hardpacked dirt road, the rhythm a quick trot, indicating the fae wasn't racing to Herstind but also wasn't on a leisurely outing. Then the horse and rider crested the hill, drew closer, and my breath caught in my aching chest.

CHAPTER 4
Sage

THE FAE LORD riding up the road was stunning. Of course, he was fae, so he was supposed to be stunning. But I'd never seen a fae before and had always assumed the stories about their beauty had been exaggerated.

His blond hair shimmered like gold in stark contrast to his all black clothing but was surprisingly short — since most tales said fae wore their hair long. Although I supposed if you were a professional soldier, long hair might be more of a hindrance than a help.

He slowed his mount, a large black stallion, and acknowledged the gate guard who gave him a curt nod then turned his attention to me, capturing me with piercing green eyes.

Except they weren't just green, they were emeralds, like the small emerald dangling from the string around

my neck. Eyes like a gem or a precious metal. Just like
the stories said. Those jeweled eyes were captured in a
sculpted, beautiful, almost boyish face, but I wasn't
foolish enough to think he was Sawyer's age or even
mine. Fae didn't age the way humans did. For all I
knew this fae was centuries old and far from naive.

"My lord," I said, sinking into a deep curtsey as he
approached, half in an attempt to avoid staring at his
eyes, or his face, or his pointed ears peeking out of his
messy golden locks, and half to hide how stunned I
was just looking at him. "Welcome to Herstind Castle,
will you require lodging?"

"No," he replied, his voice soft as he dismounted. "I
can't stay."

"See to the man's horse," I said to Dodd while
taking a step back from the fae.

He wasn't as big or as broad-shouldered as I'd
imagined — the one thing I guess the stories had
gotten wrong — but he was still a head taller than me.
Even if his face suggested he wasn't dangerous, the rest
of him with his black leather armor, the longsword at
his hip, and the two long daggers on his other hip did,
and I didn't want to risk him having the same kind of
temper as Edred's.

"Just water him. This won't take long." The fae
tossed a copper bit to Dodd, making the child's eyes
widen in surprise, and the boy bobbed, bowing
profusely in gratitude. The bit wasn't much, but Edred

barely paid his servants, and as a child, Dodd wasn't paid anything.

"That was kind, my lord," I murmured, keeping my gaze lowered because it was expected of me, but also so I wouldn't end up staring at him again. "Thank you."

I led him across the bailey to the keep's main doors while Dodd took the stallion toward the trough by the stables.

The fae didn't respond to my comment. Not that I expected him to, but when I glanced at him — unable to help myself — he didn't look bored or haughty like I'd imagined a fae lord would be at being reduced to a messenger. His posture was tight and not with just the coiled tightness of a warrior, but someone about to do something he didn't want to do.

How many towns had he already visited? How many families had he told that their son or brother or father was going to the Gray?

There were usually only a handful of men selected each year, but this might not have been this fae's first time delivering the bad news. Herstind might not be his first stop this year, and how many other years had he ridden out and delivered the news? How many times had he had to deal with crying mothers and wives and children? Even the most hardened warrior — unless he didn't have a heart — couldn't keep relaying terrible news year after year and not be affected.

"No one here will weep," I said, climbing the half dozen shallow steps to the keep's main doors.

I didn't know why I felt the need to reassure him that he could just deliver his message and be on his way, but just like looking at him, I couldn't seem to help myself.

He frowned at me and I jerked my attention away.

"What?" he asked.

"There'll be no crying women or children at Herstind." I grabbed the ring to one of the two heavy doors. "No one will argue the selection."

Not that the selection could be argued with. If the sacrifice refused to take on the spell binding him to the Black Tower, the messenger would force him. Which explained why they'd sent a fae who was greater in size and strength than a human. And even if Edred had manipulated the selection process, I still couldn't dispute it, not until I was free of him and found a way for the king to listen to me or found a way to break the binding spell. Except Sawyer was the person most likely to figure out how to break the spell and he wouldn't be able to do that at the Black Tower.

"I think no reaction is worse," the fae said. "It's best when it's a celebration—"

My gaze jumped back to his for a heart-stopping second with my shock at what he'd just said before I yanked it back down.

Why couldn't I stop looking at him?

It had to be because he was so beautiful and exotic... even though it felt more like something inside me urged me to look at him. Maybe that was his magic. Maybe he compelled people to pay attention to him, as if his stunning looks weren't enough.

"You've encountered celebrations at being the sacrifice?" I forced out, determined to keep my gaze down like Edred and the rest of society demanded.

"Not many. But there are some humans who recognize their duty to protect the Gray," he replied, his voice soft and strange, not giving me any indication how he felt about that. "I've seen families who've raised their sons to answer the call, taking the place of someone else in their city."

It seemed crazy that someone would willingly send their children to the Gray or to be raised knowing you'd never be allowed to fall in love or have a family, that you were going to spend the rest of your life as a soldier. Even when men became too old for regular duty, they remained in the Black Guard in service positions like cooking and cleaning and all the other things needed to maintain the Guard and its keep.

But I supposed that was one way to deal with a fate you had no control of. It wasn't the fate I'd choose, but I could see why someone might embrace it. Even if your destiny wasn't a normal life and possibly an early grave, at least you knew what your destiny was and didn't spend ten years praying your name was never drawn in the lottery.

"There won't be a celebration here, either," I said.

Except there probably would be. Edred had finally figured out how to get rid of Sawyer without incurring the wrath of the king's inquisitors and if someone questioned Sawyer's selection, Edred could say he was as surprised as everyone else. He could claim our mother must have forgotten to remove Sawyer's name from the lottery when our middle brother had died making Sawyer the new heir even though I knew she had. He'd also say that Sawyer's name being entered before he was of age was an accident. It was rare, but I'd heard it had happened before. Edred probably wouldn't even wait for Sawyer to leave before starting his celebrations.

I shoved that bitter thought as deep down as I could and schooled my expression. Edred was already in a foul mood and looking like the willful stepdaughter he'd hoped to have gotten rid of years ago wouldn't help.

"My lord," I said, my gaze flickering to his again despite my determination to avoid eye contact. "May I have your name."

He stared back at me and his brilliant green eyes, perhaps the most dangerous weapon on his person, stunned me all over again. "There's no need. I'm just a Guardsman."

"You're fae." I heaved my attention to his boots. They were black, like the rest of his clothing, and worn, making me wonder if the Black Guard had a dress uniform that this man wasn't wearing, or if it was practical leather armor and nothing else. "The Marquis of Herstind March, Lord Edred, will expect a proper introduction."

"So, he's one of those," the fae sighed. "Fine. I'm Quill."

I wasn't sure what he meant by "one of those" but I suspected the fae, Lord Quill, wasn't interested in ceremony, at least when it came to delivering the lottery's summons.

I pulled open the heavy door, savoring the breath of cool air from inside whispering against my skin before the heat outside devoured it, and stood aside so Lord Quill could enter first.

Inside, men lined both sides of the great hall, standing in front of the long tables and benches where they took their meals, creating an aisle that drew the eye straight to the back where Edred sat on his throne. The throne, a heavy, intricate piece of furniture that had been built after my mother had died was raised a good three feet above everyone else on a wide dais — something he'd also built after my mother's passing.

To his right and slightly behind him on a much simpler chair sat his new bride, a meek woman a few years younger than me. She sat with her hands clasped in her lap, her gaze locked on them, and her back perfectly straight. Everything about her was perfect: her clothes, her hair, and her manners. She was the perfect image of the perfect wife, beautiful, quiet, and obedient.

To his left, and a good two steps behind, stood Sawyer. He'd managed to get his breathing under control and had changed out of the heavy padded practice tunic into a white shirt and red jerkin and replaced his dusty brown pants for clean black ones. His red hair that was usually tousled — very much like Lord Quill's blond locks — had been soaked and slicked back. It was the only way to make his unruly hair presentable in Edred's opinion and wouldn't last. The second it started to dry, it would curl and before long it would be back to normal. At his left hip he wore his real longsword, not the blunt practice blade, and at his right, his dagger.

"Marquis of Herstind March, Lord Edred," I called out, and a hush fell over the room. "I present Lord Quill of the Black Guard."

Lord Quill raised his chin ever so slightly, marched to the center of the hall, and stood at attention. I hurried after him, stopping a few paces behind him and to his right. If he'd brought a servant with him, I would have waited by the door, but since he was alone, Edred expected me to take the place of Lord Quill's valet even though I was a woman.

"Well met, Lord Quill of the Black Guard," Edred said, his eyes narrowing with his displeasure, likely because Lord Quill hadn't even bowed his head in respect.

"The lottery has been drawn." Lord Quill pulled out a thin bronze medallion.

My heart pounded. Maybe I was wrong. Maybe Edred hadn't manipulated the lottery and Sawyer was safe.

But that was a childish hope. I already knew the truth. Edred hadn't even tried to hide his pleasure at hearing that a member of the Black Guard was riding up the road. Lord Quill was going to say Sawyer's name and all I could do was pray he'd survive long enough for me to figure out how to release him.

Except with Sawyer's condition, he wouldn't last a fortnight. Maybe I could go with him to the Black Tower and beg for his release. Which was a ridiculous idea.

I'd have less hope petitioning the Commander of the Black Guard than I would the king. The Black Guard was all men and only men. I had even less value in the Black Tower than I did in Herstind March. At least there were women in the Kingdom of Erellod's court who might be able to bend the king's ear on my behalf.

Of course, anyone with any sense would pull Sawyer from serious training the moment they saw his condition, which would probably be by the end of the first day. They'd know he was a liability, but that didn't mean they'd set him free. They'd assign him a service position... which might give me enough time to fix this.

Darkness fluttered across my vision and the piece of floor in front of my toes where I'd been staring vanished beneath a heavy mist. The mist curled around my ankles, bringing with it a frozen fear that snaked up my legs and wound around my heart.

My pulse shuddered. I was having a premonition.

My fear from the premonition deepened along with the worry of someone discovering that something was wrong with me.

I'd never had two premonitions within a fortnight of each other, let alone in the same day, and I couldn't let anyone know about my ability. Edred most of all. If he knew I had the ability to sense the future, he'd try to force me to use it for his personal gain. Except I had no control over my premonitions. I didn't know when the darkness would come over me or what it would warn me of. Sometimes I couldn't even figure out what it meant because all I got were vague sensations.

But in this case, I already knew Sawyer was in danger, and I didn't need my unusual instincts to remind me.

Except this premonition was so much stronger than any I'd experienced before. The others had always been darkness joined with a flash of emotion.

I'd never experience the fog before and the emotion filling me now was overwhelming.

A cold wind gusted, chilling the sweat on my body, cutting through my thin summer dress and stinging my skin as if I'd stepped through a fae ring to someplace freezing. The mist whirled around and around then opened up revealing Sawyer.

He lay at my feet, his lifeless eyes staring at nothing and his pale skin ashen. Behind him, freestanding in the mist without any sign of a wall, stood a massive black door engraved with writhing shadowy monsters. The Shadow Gate.

It was exactly like the drawing I'd seen when I was a child. Except it was so much bigger than I imagined, towering above me and stretching wide enough for at least half a dozen carriages to pass through side by side.

The fear twisted tighter and an overwhelming sense of urgency seized me. Sawyer's body was going to give out while he was in the Gray, and it was going to happen soon.

CHAPTER 5
Sage

MY HEART POUNDED and the icy fear shook me. I couldn't let Sawyer go into the Gray. I had to stop this. We had to flee—

Except there was no way we could run. Even if half of Edred's men weren't in the great hall, Lord Quill would stop us. I doubted we'd even get out of the hall, and even if we did, there was no way Sawyer would be able to run far enough, fast enough for us to escape the fae.

No, the binding spell couldn't be avoided. But the moment he stepped into the Gray, his life was in danger. I didn't have a fortnight. Everything within me said I had days and that wasn't enough time to do anything. I couldn't let Sawyer be the one bound to the Black Tower.

"Girl!" Edred barked.

I jerked my attention up, losing my balance with the sudden movement. Someone grabbed my arm, steadying me and sending a shock of something powerful and breathtaking zinging through me, and the mist and darkness vanished. My world snapped back to the great hall — although I knew I hadn't actually left — and Lord Quill held my arm while everyone stared at me.

"I said bring the summons here so Sawyer can do his duty," Edred said as he unsheathed his dagger, his gaze daring me to speak up and argue against Lord Quill's announcement... which I hadn't actually heard because I'd had a vision, an honest to goodness actual vision, not just a premonition.

"I—"

"Are you alright?" Lord Quill asked me, his voice soft and soothing and doing nothing to ease the fear still clutching my aching chest.

My gaze dropped to his hand on my arm, his grip firm and warm, almost reassuring — if a *grip* could be reassuring. I could feel the frozen mist and overwhelming fear writhing at the edge of my senses, but they couldn't get past whatever it was in Lord Quill's touch that kept me rooted in my body.

"You said his name?" The words slipped out even though I'd known what Lord Quill was going to say. A small part of me had still hoped I was wrong despite Edred's reaction to the fae's arrival and my vision.

"Yes." His expression darkened and the tightness I'd seen in his face earlier returned.

I'd promised there wouldn't be any weeping. And there wouldn't be. Sawyer wasn't dead yet and he wasn't bound to the Black Tower. He wasn't ever going to be bound to it. If anyone was going to be able to find a way to break the binding spell it would be Sawyer and he wouldn't be able to do that in the Gray. I couldn't let him go through with it, and if running away wasn't an option then someone else had to take his place.

Oh, Father! That someone had to be me.

I was the better swordsman and could withstand the rigors of training better than he could. We had the same red hair, same sharp facial features, were roughly the same size, and I doubted Lord Quill had taken a good enough look at either of us to tell the difference.

I wasn't stupid enough to think I could hide the fact that I was a woman forever, but all I needed was to hide long enough for Sawyer to get as far away from the Five Great Kingdoms as possible. After that, I could beg for the Lord Commander's mercy or hope Sawyer found a way to break or block the binding spell so I could escape.

Maybe if I was really lucky, I'd be able to keep my secret until Sawyer came of age and was able to petition the king without needing to go through Edred first.

"Girl," Edred snapped again.

I bowed my head and bit my lip, reopening the wound Edred had given me so I could dab my blood on the medallion and complete the binding spell.

If the text I'd read about the spell was correct, there were no outward signs that the spell had been awakened or that someone was bound to the Black Tower. Only the recipient felt the spell sealing his fate. He would be compelled within a few days to go to the Gray or the spell would slowly start to drain his life, eventually killing him.

"Bring the summons," Edred snarled, his tone clear that my disobedience was going to be punished and every second I hesitated the punishment grew worse.

"Yes, my lord." I swiped my thumb over my bleeding lip then took the medallion with my other hand. I didn't want to chance Lord Quill seeing the blood on my thumb and thinking I was pressing my blood on the medallion by accident.

This was a terrible plan.

But the other option was letting Sawyer die — and without a doubt, he'd die. My premonitions always came true, and this premonition was the strongest I'd ever had. Pretending to be Sawyer was the only way to save him.

I turned away from Lord Quill to face Edred, and cupped my hands together, brushing my bloody thumb against the edge of the medallion as I walked down the aisle.

Sudden heat swept over my hand. It burned around my wrist and up my forearm to my elbow, bringing with it a searing, fiery agony that made me stumble.

I bit back a gasp and fought to keep my balance. The heat burned hotter and I dipped my head down, hoping I looked obedient and not like I was in pain and forced myself to keep walking.

Slow and steady. Don't let anyone see how much it hurts.

But it felt like I'd shoved my arm into a fire and was holding it there. Thankfully, just like the text had promised, my flesh looked perfectly normal, which meant so long as I managed to keep a straight face, no one would know the truth.

I reached the edge of Edred's dais, dropped into a low curtsey — grateful the movement hid my trembling — and held out the medallion, presenting it to Edred. "The summons, my lord."

Edred's lips curled back in a sneer and he held out his dagger to Sawyer. "Make it quick. I don't have all day."

"Yes, my lord." Sawyer took the dagger, pierced the tip of his finger, and marched down the three steps to stand in front of me.

I raised my gaze to meet his and prayed he'd see

the silent plea in my eyes. *Please understand and accept this. It's the only way. Please don't draw attention to this.* He was smart. He'd catch on right away to what I'd done. He had to.

He pressed his bloody fingertip against the medallion and frowned, clearly not feeling the burn of the spell and knowing instantly that something was wrong.

"Look like your arm hurts," I whispered.

His eyes widened in shock. "Sage, you didn't." He drew in a breath to argue — it was foolish to think he wouldn't argue about this — but I jerked my gaze over his shoulder to Edred.

"Not in front of Edred. He'll be furious we messed this up." We could argue later, although there wasn't really that much to argue about. The spell had been completed and the only way to deal with it was to go to the Black Tower. Right now, we needed to get out of the great hall and away from Edred and his men and finish solidifying my foolish, barely formed plan. "Please."

CHAPTER 6

Sage

SAWYER'S EYES narrowed and he gripped his arm and left out a strangle grunt, making Edred's smile turned predatory.

"Thank you, Lord Quill," Edred practically purred and my traitorous gaze slid back to the handsome fae. "Will you join us for the evening meal and stay the night?"

"No." Lord Quill's emerald eyes locked with mine for a breathtaking moment then he turned on his heel and strode out of the hall.

"See him off, girl," Edred barked, and I scrambled to catch up with him, my arm still throbbing from the spell and my bruised chest aching with each breath.

Lord Quill was already a third of the way across the bailey by the time I'd raced down the aisle and out the large main door, his stride long and fast as if he couldn't wait to get out of Herstind castle, something I couldn't blame him for.

"My lord," I called out, although I wasn't sure what to say after that.

I couldn't arrange to have his horse saddled, since it already was, and there was nothing else I could offer him. It seemed idiotic to thank him for coming like Edred expected of me. I'd almost lost Sawyer because of him and I was about to take the largest gamble of my life.

Except that wasn't fair. It wasn't his fault Edred had manipulated the lottery and ensured Sawyer's name was drawn.

Lord Quill glanced back at me, his expression stiff. "I can't change the results of the lottery."

"I know." I dropped into a low curtsy, fighting to keep my gaze down, but just like before, my eyes lifted as if compelled by him. "This duty can't be easy. Thank you for your service."

Some of the tension melted from his gaze and for a moment I saw a glimmer of a brilliant, kind man — and I had no idea if I was actually seeing him or having another strange premonition.

"It's not so bad," he said, his tone softening. "Your brother's life—" He frowned. "Or your cousin or whoever he is to you."

"My brother," I replied. The only member of my family I had left.

"His life won't be what he'd planned," Lord Quill said, turning and continuing to march toward his horse, "but life in the Guard isn't all bad. He's lost a sister, and for that I'm sorry, but he's gained three hundred brothers."

Three hundred? I knew the Guard was more than just a handful of men, but I hadn't expected there to be three hundred.

A shudder swept through me. I had to convince three hundred men that I was one of them?

Maybe that would be easier than just trying to convince a few.

If I didn't draw attention to myself — more attention than my red hair already drew — I could find a way to make it work at least until Sawyer had enough time to flee beyond the borders of the Five Great Kingdoms and hide.

We reached the stables at the far end of the bailey. Dodd was nowhere to be seen, which didn't surprise me given how terrified the boy had been of Lord Quill, and the fae didn't seem to care. He released his horse from the hitching post and swung up into the saddle.

"He won't need to come to the tower until tomorrow. Noon at the latest," Lord Quill said. "You have time for a proper goodbye."

"Thank you," I murmured, knowing he expected a response — and the truth that Sawyer and I would likely have to leave the castle immediately wasn't something he needed to hear.

"Miss," he said, addressing me as a maid, not realizing I was nobility because of the dirt on my clothes and how Edred had treated me.

He dipped his head in goodbye, the first time during his visit that he'd shown anyone respect, and I was grateful Edred wasn't around to witness it.

With that he urged his horse into a trot and rode out of the castle. I watched him go, my traitorous eyes still searching him out, waiting for him to disappear down the slope in the road, before the compulsion released me. Then I turned back to the keep and drew in a steadying breath of hot, humid air as Sawyer hurried across the bailey toward me.

Whether it was foolish or not, I'd made a decision and now I had to go through with it.

"What's wrong with you?" Sawyer hissed, his breath wet and rattling in his chest. "Have you lost your mind? We have to stop him and tell him there's been a mistake. If we're lucky we can convince him not to say anything to Edred."

He turned to run out the gate, but I grabbed his arm and yanked him back to face me.

"We're not doing anything. I doubt Lord Quill can break the binding spell which means he'd have to tell Edred because both of us would have to go to the Black Tower."

Sawyer wrenched his arm out of my grip. "Better to be beaten by Edred for embarrassing him than you joining the Black Guard."

"Better me than you. You wouldn't survive a day in the Gray."

"You're a girl!"

"And the better swordsman," I shot back.

One of Edred's men strode across the bailey toward us and I ducked my head, trying to look demure and praying he hadn't overheard our argument even though we'd kept our voices low.

"Lord Edred says your lesson in obedience isn't done," he said over his shoulder, as he walked past us, heading toward the guard post at the main gate. "He expects to see you in his chambers."

My pulse skipped a beat. I'd hoped Sawyer becoming a sacrifice would have been enough to please Edred into forgetting about me, but that had been a foolish hope. I'd embarrassed him twice today, once in front of Pylos when I'd interrupted Sawyer's lesson, and again in the great hall in front of half of his men when I'd hesitated to bring him the medallion. I'd been punished for less and if I made him wait, the beating would be worse. But if I obeyed him, there was a chance he'd lock me up for days and the binding spell would kill me.

I grabbed Sawyer's sleeve and yanked him back toward the keep. "We have to go. Right now."

"You're not going anywhere. You're a girl." He wrenched his sleeve free. "Do you know what they'll do to you if they learn the truth?"

"Hopefully kick me out of the Black Guard," I seized his wrist again and started pulling him back toward the keep. "We can't stay here."

"Or they'll keep you around as the Tower whore," he replied with a wheezing cough.

"Don't be ridiculous." I dragged him along the edge of the keep, heading toward the back and an entrance where we were least likely to run into Edred. "They don't keep women at the Black Tower, not even whores." It was more likely I'd be sent to court to face the king and be charged with disobeying the crown and imprisoned for the rest of my life for circumventing the lottery.

"Someone is going to find out. How are you going to bathe? What about sleeping? Soldiers are bunked in cots in one big room." He yanked out of my grip just before we rounded the corner. "Sage, this isn't supposed to be your destiny."

"It's not yours, either." He was all I had left and I wasn't going to let Edred send him to his death. And while I could tell him I'd foreseen his death, he'd just say he'd be more careful. Except I knew with all of my being that being careful wouldn't be enough to change what I'd seen.

"You could have petitioned the king, not taken the

binding spell," he insisted. "I'm heir to Herstind March and not even sixteen. It's obvious someone's made a mistake."

I set my hands on my hips and glared at him. "You don't really believe it was just a mistake."

He glared back at me then sighed and ran his hands through his drying hair, making the red locks stick out at odd angles. "No. It took me a moment to realize Edred was far too happy at the fae lord's arrival. I knew walking into the great hall that my name was going to be on the summons."

"Which means Edred has significant influence on the men administering the lottery, possibly even the head magistrate." For all I knew, he had the king's ear. He'd been one of His Majesty's generals until he'd married our mother and took over the defense of the March.

That thought sent a new fear rushing through me.

"Or he's got the king's ear," Sawyer said as if he'd read my thoughts. And if that was the case, there wasn't anything either of us could do to stop Edred's plan to get rid of Sawyer.

CHAPTER 7

Sage

SAWYER'S EYES widened with realization. "I might not be able to petition the king to free you from the Black Tower without you being severely punished or be able to convince him that my name had been drawn in error. If he truly is Edred's ally, then we'll both end up in prison or dead."

"Which means our only way out of this is for you to find a way to break the binding spell." I grabbed his arm, urging him to start moving again. "And we can't do that here. We need to get to your room, get supplies, and get into the tunnel before Edred sends someone to fetch me."

"Except I can't remove the binding spell," he said, trying to keep up with me and catch his breath as we rounded the corner to the back of the keep.

Udara, still sitting on the kitchen step, watched us

approach. She dropped a clean potato in the bucket beside her and picked up another one, but I couldn't tell from her expression if she'd heard the news or not. It had only been a few minutes at most and both Dodd and me — the people Edred usually used to run messages — were busy. That, and even if it broke her heart that Sawyer's name had been drawn and she knew it was wrong, she wouldn't speak up against Edred. No one would.

"My lord," she said, bowing her head at Sawyer while still scrubbing her potato.

"Udara," Sawyer replied as we hurried inside, stepping out of the oppressive heat into a just as hot kitchen then beyond into a cooler, dimly lit, servants' stairwell.

We hurried up the stairs to Sawyer's room and rushed inside.

"I'm not a sorcerer," he said, continuing the conversation Udara's presence had interrupted. "I can't break a fae spell."

"But you're smart and you have a knack for finding obscure pieces of information." If my strange ability was a heightened intuition, Sawyer's was accidentally discovering just that perfect, obscure detail to baffle his tutors. "If anyone can find a way to break or circumvent the binding spell, it's you."

I opened the large trunk at the foot of his bed,

pulled out his rucksack, and shoved in two shirts, two pairs of pants, and Sawyer's old, worn, brown jerkin.

"It's more likely I'll be able to figure out who Edred coerced into manipulating the lottery results."

I jerked my attention to him. "Don't you dare. If Edred's influence goes all the way to His Majesty, the second you show your face in court, even if you wait until you're of age and no longer need Edred's help to approach the king, you'll be imprisoned or killed."

"So what?" he asked. "I just run away?"

"Right now. Yes. You run away until it no longer makes sense for the Black Guard to come after you once they discover the truth." I rummaged to the bottom of the trunk, pulled out the short sword and dagger Sawyer had been given when he was a child then grabbed his old pair of boots and his cloak and shoved them into his arms. "Now come on."

We rushed back into the hall and down the servants' stairs, stopping just out of sight at the bottom. A quick glance around the corner confirmed no one was in the kitchen and Udara still sat on the step scrubbing potatoes with her back turned to us.

With a jerk of my chin, I indicated it was all clear, just like I used to when we were children and were sneaking into the kitchen to steal Udara's freshly baked tarts. But instead of taking tarts, Sawyer wrapped the handful of apples, the half-eaten loaf of bread, and the chunk of cheese sitting on the countertop in his cloak, and I grabbed a candle and holder and lit the wick in the kitchen's fire. Then we hurried down the stairs into the cellar and went straight to the narrow wooden door at the back that was partially hidden behind a stack of barrels.

A heavy wooden beam secured the door against outside intruders, and I handed Sawyer the candle-holder and set down the weapons and rucksack so I could lift the beam with both hands and try to silently set it on the floor.

Thankfully, I didn't make much noise as I struggled with the beam, and I tucked it against the wall as out of sight as possible and gathered my things. We wouldn't be able to secure the door after we left, but the moment Edred realized we were gone and hadn't left by the main gate, he'd know we slipped out through the tunnel.

I could only pray that it would take him a while to figure out what had happened, that no one would accidentally notice that the bar on the tunnel door had been removed, and that we'd have enough time to get to Olinon and use the fae ring.

Once we'd gone through the ring, the only way Edred would know where we'd gone was if someone in the village had watched us leave. And I was hoping even if someone did, their dislike of Edred and their love for our mother and father would protect us... at least until we'd taken a second ring to another location.

Knowing the hinges on the door creaked, I slowly eased the door open.

Inside lay a long narrow staircase, the steps, walls, and ceiling smooth, carved from the stone Herstind castle sat on.

I didn't know why the tunnel had been originally built. If the castle was under siege, it was a serious weakness in its defenses, but I'd been told it had been built as a means of escape for women and children — or in Edred's case, Edred himself — in the event that a siege had turned dire or the main gate had been breached.

Sawyer, still holding the candle went first, his partially swallowed coughs making the flame tremble. His pace was slower than I liked but it was as fast as I knew he could handle without completely losing his breath.

The air was cool, nothing like the cold I'd felt from the mist in my vision, but it reminded me of what I'd seen.

I didn't know how I'd actually seen it, but I knew in every fiber of my being that it was true... or would have been true if Sawyer had become a member of the Black Guard. What I didn't know was how I'd seen it in the first place or what it might mean.

I'd had premonitions since I was a child. A sense of dread would overwhelm me and leave me wondering what was going to happen and when. Everyone said I just had a nervous disposition, but then the dread turned into a vague knowing, a storm was coming, the brigands were going to attack a nearby village, the winter's yearly sweating sickness would be worse than usual.

I'd kept it a secret for fear someone would claim I was fae-touched and send me to the king to be used like the handful of other fae-touched humans discovered in Erellod. And when mother had married Edred, I tried even harder to keep my ability a secret, knowing he wouldn't hand me over to His Majesty, he'd keep me for himself.

Over the last couple of years, the premonitions had grown stronger and more frequent, and the sense of what and when had also grown stronger. But I'd never actually *seen* anything before, and now I couldn't make myself stop seeing Sawyer's lifeless eyes staring into nothing, the cold mist swirling around him, and the Shadow Gate towering above him.

I hugged the rucksack tighter as if it would help keep me warm against the cool air. I was going into that mist and going to see that gate in person. I was going to have to lie and pray I could keep lying until Sawyer had left the Five Great Kingdoms and had gotten as far away from any fae ring as possible, and I had no idea if I could actually do that.

CHAPTER 8

Sage

W E REACHED the bottom of the stairs and stepped onto ground that was just as smooth as the stairwell, the tunnel ceiling rising high above us. There was nothing natural about this tunnel and I couldn't even begin to imagine the amount of work necessary to carve the stairs and passage. Unless, of course, a fae had helped. If the rumors of their magic were true, a fae gifted with the magic to manipulate the earth could have molded the stone around us with just a thought.

Sawyer's breathing was already starting to sound strained, and it was getting harder for him to control his coughing, but he pressed onward. The tunnel ran a fair distance away from Herstind castle, but he knew as well as I did that once Edred realized what we'd done, he'd send riders to the tunnel's entrance and men down the stairs to stop us. Our only advantage was that the ground between the castle and the entrance was rough and the horses would have to go the long way around to get to it. That and we probably had at least a little bit of time before Edred started searching the keep for either of us.

Except if Sawyer kept going as he was, he wouldn't make it to Olinon. He'd collapse first.

I grabbed his shirt sleeve, giving it a gentle tug. "Slow down a bit."

"We have to keep moving," he insisted, maintaining his pace and making my insides squirm.

Yes. We did. *Now now now.* We couldn't get caught. But—

"If you collapse, we won't be moving at all. We still have a bit of time before Edred realizes we're missing." And I prayed that was the truth. "We can get to the ring in Olinon before he does."

"You honestly think he won't follow us through the ring?" he asked, but he did slow his pace a little, filling me with a churning mix of fear that we weren't moving fast enough and worry that the pace was still too fast for him.

"If we're lucky, no one will see where we went," I replied.

He huffed. "I wouldn't want to bet on that. It'll be best to go to Gastow then go somewhere else."

"Do you honestly think Gastow is actually abandoned or the ring still works?"

Last winter a traveling minstrel had stayed at Herstind castle and told us tales about the abandoned mining village in the Gastanovian mountains. The minstrel had made it sound like no one knew why the village had been abandoned, but the best guess was that they'd taken whatever they could from the mountain and had moved on, or the wasting sickness killed most of the villagers and those who survived had left.

"Let's hope so," he said. "Once we're there, we can turn around and go someplace else. Edred might be able to follow us to Gastow but there won't be anyone around to see where we go after that."

"And you remember the pattern to connect the ring?" The minstrel had only mentioned it once, and I wasn't sure how well Sawyer had been listening to him. Quizzical tales and mysteries appealed to him, but not tales of adventure, and the minstrel's story had been a bit of both.

"Of course I remember the pattern. I remember the pattern to almost every known ring in the Five Great Kingdoms."

And I had no doubt he did. If it involved something intellectual, he remembered it. If it involved the physical, he was hopeless.

I, on the other hand, had been barely adequate in my studies — at least until Edred had dismissed my tutor and I'd become just another maid. It had always been difficult to sit and listen. I needed to move and always had to fight the call of the outside, even in the height of summer and the depth of winter.

Ahead, hints of light cut through the thick under-brush hiding the tunnel's mouth, and we paused long enough to listen and look for signs that Edred had beaten us there.

The forest was quiet, or as quiet as it normally got with the gentle wind rustling through the leaves and birds chirping. Sunlight streamed through the thick canopy with great slashes of light and while it was still cooler beneath the trees compared to standing in the middle of the bailey without shade, I could still feel the summer's heat radiating against my skin in contrast to the tunnel's cool dampness.

I took a little longer than normal to check our surroundings to give Sawyer time to catch his breath, all the while my mind screaming that we couldn't stop, we didn't have any time to wait. Then we hurried through the underbrush to a nearby game trail. It would be faster and easier to take the road, but that would also make it easier for Edred's men to catch us. That, and we'd have to climb up the rocky slope that currently protected us from an easy capture to get to it.

I let Sawyer set our pace despite the fear twisting my insides. After reminding him that collapsing wouldn't help us, he kept to a steady march, but even then, he was gasping and coughing by the time we broke through the underbrush into the large clearing just outside of Olinon where the fae ring sat.

The ring, a large silver and bronze circle that was partially buried in the ground, was wide enough for a carriage to pass through. Swirly fae writing traced up one side of the arc, stretching from my knees to my head, and while I didn't know what it said, I knew pressing the words in different combinations linked the ring's magic to other rings across the Great Five Kingdoms joined in the human-fae treaty to defend the Gates of the Realms.

It sat about fifty yards from the town's tall, wooden wall, and about a hundred yards from us. The town's gates were wide open, inviting in what little trade that came through the ring and up the road, and I could see all the way through from one open gate to the other and the couple dozen people inside going about their business despite it being the hottest hours of the day.

My pulse raced and sweat plastered my dress to my back. Sawyer, sweat also dripping down his forehead, started to slow, each gasp sounding harder than the last.

"Just a little farther," I said, grabbing his arm and tugging him along.

"I know—" He stumbled and I caught him.

Fire flickered up my arm — the arm that had the spell binding me to the Black Tower — and I fought to ignore the sensation. It was just a remnant of the magic that had swept into me when the spell had been awakened. I was sure I'd be feeling flickers of that fire for days.

But as we got closer to the ring, the heat grew stronger. It burned over my hand and up my forearm, growing just as painful as the first time it had blazed into me. When we were a dozen steps away, white light flared from four of the words on the ring, and the fire in my arm surged.

"Someone's coming through," Sawyer gasped.

"No," I forced out between clenched teeth. "It's the binding spell." It had to be.

Lord Quill hadn't given Sawyer the pattern to connect to the ring in the Gray, and very few people knew the pattern. Which meant the pattern had to be part of the binding spell, a way of guaranteeing sacrifices couldn't avoid their duty by using the rings. "It's activated the ring."

Sawyer swore. "If you move away, will the ring go back to sleep?"

He pushed out of my arms and I took a step back. The words still glowed.

Damn. Would the ring stay like that until I'd stepped through? If Sawyer and I went through into the Gray, would we be able to travel somewhere else right away or would we be stuck there? I didn't know if the ring in the Gray had magic that restricted who could use it. The binding spell might kill someone if they left the Black Tower, but was there another level of security to stop the sacrifices from leaving without permission.

I took another step back and another while Sawyer hurried forward to the ring. The fire in my arm dimmed then flickered and went out, and so did the light in the ring.

Sawyer frowned at me. I was all the way to the edge of the clearing again and was going to have to run when Sawyer entered the pattern for Gastow to make it to the ring before it went back to sleep.

"Let's see if it will stay connected to the ring in Gastow or if when I come closer, it switches back to the Gray," I called out.

Sawyer opened his mouth to respond, but the sound of hooves pounding up the road stopped him. His eyes widened. There was no time to check to see if the binding spell would change the connection or even to see if this ring could connect with the ring in Gastow. We had to go now.

"Do it," I said, fighting to stay where I was until Sawyer had completed the pattern.

Sawyer pressed the pattern, making white light flare around the words and his hand. Then the light blossomed in the center of the ring, a small white flower that slowly unfurled and grew.

The pounding hooves drew closer and Pylos galloped around the bend in the road.

I didn't have time to wait for the spell to fully encompass the ring. I wouldn't make it there before Pylos came into the clearing.

The ring had connected to the ring in Gastow — or the ring's magic wouldn't have blossomed to life — and I just had to pray the spell wouldn't jump to the ring in the Gray once I was close.

I barreled toward the ring, my attention locked on the glowing words at its edge. The binding spell in my arm exploded into fiery agony and Pylos yelled at us to stop. Light flickered through all the words in the ring and the flower in the center of the ring flared brighter, filling the entire space with blinding light.

"Get back here, girl," Pylos yelled, charging toward me.

He leaned in his saddle, grabbed a handful of my hair, and jerked me back as Sawyer leaped through and disappeared. Except I had no idea if he'd gone through to Gastow or into the Gray and had to get free of Pylos to follow before the ring went back to sleep.

CHAPTER 9
Sage

I TWISTED, Pylos's grasp painfully pulling at my hair, and bashed my still-sheathed short sword against his hand as hard as I could. With a yelp, he let go and I dove through the ring after Sawyer.

The magic of the ring tingled over my skin, sweeping from my head to my feet as I passed through, then my head and right shoulder slammed against something solid.

The world lurched around me, flickering to darkness for a second before clearing to a slightly-spinning, cloudy day.

Large, uneven stones crowded to my right, partially covering the ring and blocking most of the path in front of it. To my left was a sharp drop, too close to the ring to have been there when the ring had first been built, and above towered white-capped peaks. A stinging wind swept down the mountainside, gusting over my skin in a sudden, shocking contrast to the oppressive summer heat in Herstind where we'd just been.

Sawyer grabbed my arm and hauled me to my feet. "You have to get away so I can connect to another gate before Pylos gets—"

The light in the ring shuddered, and Pylos rode through just as the magic vanished.

My pulse lurched. He'd made it just before the original connection had broken.

His horse reared, dancing uneasily in the suddenly tight space, and he fought to control the beast as my mind raced.

I couldn't win a fight against Pylos. He was bigger and stronger than me and an experienced soldier. We had to leave. Now. Except with the space around the ring so tight, there was no way we'd be able to enter another address and go through without him following.

It would be best to run and hide. Which a horrible plan. We didn't know the area, and I hadn't even gotten a good look around us to know if running was even an option.

No. I was going to have to fight him and I was going to have to win.

And the first thing I needed to do was get him off his horse. He had a greater reach than me with both his longer sword and arms, and on top of that, being mounted gave him a serious advantage.

I lunged for him just as Sawyer leaped in as well. Except Sawyer flapped his cloak at the horse's eyes, sending the food he'd taken from the kitchen flying in all directions.

The horse reared up and Pylos jerked back to avoid my grasp. Then his eyes widened with sudden surprise, and I realized he was off balance.

With a scream, I swung my still-sheathed short sword against his hands, breaking his grip on the reins and he fell off the horse, crashing onto the uneven rocky ground, and tumbled over the cliff's edge.

His wild, desperate scream cut through the silence, making my stomach lurch, and my thoughts stuttered at the abrupt end to the fight.

It had happened so fast.

One moment we were struggling for our lives. The next it was over.

On instinct, I grabbed the horse's reins so it wouldn't bolt and hurt itself, and, with Sawyer's help, fought to control its head until it stopped panicking. A grim part of me wanted to check for Pylos's body to confirm he was actually dead, but it was foolish to try without calming the horse first. And even as I thought that, I realized my arm burned and white light was forming in the center of the ring.

The horse heaved against our grip, but we held tight until it calmed, huffing and shaking its head, still distressed but no longer panicking. I pressed a firm hand over its nose, and murmured soothing words, as Sawyer gathered the food that had fallen out of his cloak then turned to the ring, fully lit and ready to take me to the Gray.

"You have to step back," he said between wracking coughs as he wrapped the food and his old boots in his cloak so he only had one thing to carry. He held the bundle out to me and an apple to the horse. "I've got Bayard."

I took his cloak and gave him the reins, then climbed over a large rock and around a few others to reach a wide, flat strip that curved around the edge of the mountain. It had probably been the road leading from the ring to Gastow, but the magic in the ring vanished before I reached the curve and could see what lay beyond.

As much as I was curious, we needed to go through the gate before anyone else came through — and as much as I hadn't noticed anyone else with Pylos, I wasn't going to bet he was the only one who'd seen where we'd gone.

Sawyer pressed the words in a pattern I didn't

recognize, not taking us to one of the few ring patterns I was familiar with, which was probably good. Edred knew the patterns I did, but he didn't know all of the patterns Sawyer had memorized. And while Sawyer hadn't travelled through the rings a lot and likely hadn't been to wherever we were going, he probably remembered some detail from a book or a tale someone told and had a good guess what we might be stepping into.

White light blossomed in the ring and I hurried back to Sawyer, reaching him by the time the light fully filled the ring. We stepped through into another clearing, almost two hundred feet away from the tall stone walls of a town that had to be three times as large as Olinon.

A merchant from the Southern Isles in a bright, colorful tunic, a beautiful contrast to his dark skin, watched us step through. Beside him was a draft horse harnessed to a half-full cart, the contents hidden beneath an oiled blanket, but I knew from the one time a Southern Isles merchant had visited the keep when I was a child, he probably had colorful silks and sweet-smelling oils.

The merchant's expression was bored, but his gaze followed us as we turned away from the town and headed down the road until the last of the magic had flickered out of the ring and it was his turn to use it.

I hurried us along as quickly as I could without it looking like we were running from something. I didn't want to risk the binding spell reawakening the ring before the merchant could use it.

Thankfully, the fire in my arm only flickered for a moment after the magic in the ring had gone out then dimmed completely and the ring remained asleep. The merchant entered his pattern, light once again filling the circle, and stepped through, his draft horse lumbering behind him, pulling the heavy cart.

The moment the merchant was gone, Sawyer led me and the horse off the road with the confidence of someone who knew where he was going despite the fact he'd never been wherever we were.

We pushed through the underbrush, weaving between large trees, leaving a trail that even an apprentice huntsman could follow. It made my pulse pound despite knowing that no one knew where we'd gone.

The ground started to slope, but not enough to make it difficult for the horse, and then the underbrush opened up, revealing a narrow, rocky bank and a small stream. Sunlight sparkled in its quick-moving water and birds chittered at us, telling us we'd disturbed their peace.

We were a good couple hundred yards from the road and with thick bushes crowding behind us, along with the rise at our backs, we were well out of sight. There was still a chance someone would come to the stream to fish — or in the case of children, to play — but we were as out of the way as we could get without actually crawling into a cave.

"How did you know this was here?" I asked, as he loosely wrapped the horse's reins around a thick branch, giving it enough slack that it could munch on the leaves in front of it or drink from the stream.

"It's on the Caldensian maps," he said, still struggling to breathe from our wild escape but thankfully not coughing as much. He sat on the bank and took his cloak from me. "We should eat something."

I stared at him. "You looked at that map at least four years ago."

He quirked an eyebrow and gave me his driest look, reminding me that he remembered the strangest things despite however long ago he learned them.

"Here." He picked up the half-eaten loaf of bread, ripped off a chunk, and handed it to me.

"They'll feed me at the Black Tower." I sat beside him, setting the rucksack and weapons on the ground beneath my feet, and stared at the stream. "You won't know the next time you'll be able to eat."

"They might not feed you if they find out you're a girl."

Now it was my turn to give him a dry look.

"All right, probably not," he replied and he, too, turned his attention to the stream.

We stared at the water, an awkward silence filling the air around us.

In the blink of an eye, everything had changed. Life hadn't been easy for us at the castle, but we'd known what to expect, knew that Edred would lose his temper over the smallest things, or that Udara would keep two tarts in the kitchen for us instead of sending all of them to Edred and his men. We knew the heat of Herstind in the summer and the wet cold in the winter.

It was all we'd really known. I'd had a few more glimpses of the rest of the kingdom, travelling with our mother and father and then just our mother a little bit, mostly to the capital, but Sawyer had only had a handful of years when he'd been old enough to remember leaving Herstind and had only been to the capital once before mother married Edred.

And while Sawyer had read about the world outside of Herstind March and probably remembered every little detail, there was a huge difference between what was in a book and real life.

The memory of Pylos's scream as he fell to his death sent a shudder racing through me. I'd dreamed of becoming a Sayorian Shieldmaiden, first when I was younger and then as a wild plan in the event Sawyer's attempt to get Herstind from Edred failed.

But shieldmaidens were warrior women. They fought in battles, protected the people and the Queen of Sayoria. They killed people. I hadn't really known what that meant until now. Could I really survive as a member of the Black Guard? If the Shadow Gate opened, I'd be expected to fight and kill, and now that I was sitting still, with time to think, the fear and shock of what happened trembled within me.

I'd killed someone.

And I'd do it again if it meant protecting Sawyer.

CHAPTER 10
Sage

"How long do you honestly think you'll be able to hide who you really are?" Sawyer asked, his voice barely audible over the stream's soft burbling as if he, too, was finally realizing everything that had just happened.

"I don't know." But I needed to hold out as long as I could for Sawyer's sake. "I'll keep it up for as long as I can, but you need to get as far away from Erellod and the other kingdoms as fast as you can."

I sucked in a steadying breath. I couldn't turn back and there was no point in avoiding the inevitable. This was the path I'd been thrown onto and I would face it head on.

I unsheathed Sawyer's old dagger. It wasn't particularly sharp or as long as his new one since it belonged to the set he'd had as a child, but it would do. I could put a proper edge on it and his old sword when I got to the Black Tower. Right now, I needed it to cut my dress into strips. I liked the dress, but I was going to need to flatten my thankfully small breasts, and the dress was the only thing available that I could sacrifice.

Sawyer held out his new dagger before I could cut into the fabric. "It'll be easier with this."

"Thanks." I took the offered blade and worked on cutting a wide strip from the bottom of my dress, shortening it from my ankles to mid-calf.

"If you're going to be me, you should have my weapons." He unbuckled his sword belt and set it, with his sheathed sword and the empty dagger sheath, on the ground beside me. "I'd make you wear my most recent pair of boots as well, but I suspect the old pair will fit you better. If that fae lord was paying even the slightest attention, he'd know by where I stood behind Edred and from my clothes that I wasn't just a servant."

"I'm sure he just saw the red hair. That's all anyone sees." Except a part of me was afraid he'd remember more than just our red hair, that he'd remember me and the things I'd said to him.

"Anyone *human*," Sawyer said. "We've never met a fae before. For all we know, his magic might have something to do with remembering everything."

"I doubt that's the case and even if it is, there isn't anything we can do about it." I finished cutting the first strip then cut another, shortening my dress to my knees.

Once I'd cut the second strips, I made Sawyer turn his back, grabbed the rucksack with Sawyer's clothes and hid behind some bushes. I quickly shrugged out of the dress and, for a moment, just stared at the massive red bruise blossoming across my torso from my left ribs up to the middle of my chest.

Edred could have seriously hurt me, and it was either his skill at knowing just how much force he needed to hurt but not break bone or dumb luck that I hadn't cracked any ribs. Then my gaze slid to my pendant and the small emerald captured in gold filigree.

It was possible a man might have a fine piece of jewelry, a token of affection from a lover he had to leave behind, but it would draw attention. And while I could probably keep it hidden beneath my shirt, there was always a chance something would happen, and it would slip out.

That, and as much as it was now the only thing I had left of our mother, it would be better to give it to Sawyer to sell. I'd have food and lodging at the Black Tower. I couldn't go anywhere and had no need for money. Sawyer, however, had nothing but the clothes he currently wore.

If he was going to travel out of the Five Great King-doms, he'd need money. And while he could sell the horse — and should definitely sell his red jerkin so he wouldn't stand out anymore than he already did with his red hair — selling the necklace would be best.

My heart hurt and tears of frustration — that I was grateful Sawyer couldn't see — stung my eyes.

Everything would have been fine if mother hadn't married Edred. Except she hadn't had a choice. Women weren't allowed to hold land. She wouldn't have been able to keep Herstind March for Sawyer if she hadn't remarried after our father had died.

She could have fostered us with other nobles and become a temple maiden for the Great Father, but that would have meant renouncing her title and the king would have given the March to someone else. And if my greatest fear was true that the king was involved in Sawyer's name being drawn in the lottery, then the March would have still ended up in Edred's control.

And I'd be damned to the darkest shadows if I was going to let Edred remain the Marquis of Herstind March. I didn't know how I'd unseat him, especially trapped at the Black Tower — or worse in prison for taking Sawyer's place among the Guard — but I would make it happen.

And that meant not standing around — naked! — feeling sorry for myself.

I hurriedly wrapped the strips around my breasts as tight as I could bare with my aching chest. I was going to have to experiment with how I wrapped them so I could still move properly and breathe while not looking like a girl, but for now, I just needed to get through the rest of the day and not draw suspicion the moment I stepped through the ring into the Gray.

For once my unfemininely small breasts were in my favor and could barely be seen once I'd pulled on Sawyer's shirt. And with his old, worn jerkin, they were completely hidden, along with most of the curve of my hips.

Now changed, I shoved the ruined dress into the rucksack so I could finish cutting it up later and stepped out from behind the bush.

"You still look like a girl," he said, giving my long hair a pointed look as I took off my soft leather shoes and shoved them in the rucksack then pulled on Sawyer's old boots.

"Of course I do." I rolled my eyes at him, knelt, and held out his dagger. "Now help me cut it. It needs to look like yours and I don't have a mirror."

He took the dagger and selected a lock. "There's no going back from this."

"There wasn't from the moment I took the binding spell," I replied.

"I'll find a way to break it." He cut the lock and dropped the long strands into the stream.

"And don't you dare try to figure out how high Edred's influence goes," I said, as he cut another handful of hair. "You run as far away as you can. Sell that red jerkin. The fabric is too fine and the color too distinctive. But keep the horse."

"Yes, Mother," he replied, but without any of the exasperation he usually had when I told him what to do.

"And take this." I drew the string holding my pendant over my head and held it out to him.

"I'm not taking your pendant." He cut off another chunk of hair.

"You'll need money."

"No." He dropped more hair into the stream.

"She'd understand. She'd want us to survive. She'd want you to take your rightful title and take care of the people of Herstind." I shook my head at him, the movement strange and light. I'd never cut my hair before, and it was disconcerting to feel the air against the back of my neck. "You can't do that if you're starving or if you die from the sweating sickness because you didn't have enough money for shelter during the winter."

His eyes grew glassy and for a moment I was reminded of how young he was. He wasn't even a man, not yet sixteen. He'd lost so much already, our parents, our brother, and now his home.

I pressed the pendant into his hand. "You can do this."

He swallowed and slipped the string over his head and hid the pendant beneath his shirt and jerkin.

Then he cut away some final tufts of hair and handed me the dagger.

I sheathed it and secured his sword belt around my waist. We returned to the road and headed back to the ring in silence.

The ring was half lit up with two men waiting to step through, and we ducked back behind the underbrush until the area was empty.

"Put your cloak on, hide your hair, and get out of the Five Great Kingdoms," I said, pulling him into a firm hug. The Five Kingdoms were on good terms with the much younger kingdoms to our east and our north and it should be easy for him to cross the border without drawing too much attention. From there, he needed to head west or south. "You're smart, can read, and do numbers. You should be able to find work as a bookkeeper or scribe."

He hugged me back and nodded against my shoulder.

"But don't take work as a tutor. Only noble houses hire tutors and there's a chance someone could recognize you."

"Yes, Mother," he said again, his arms still wrapped around me.

"Now go."

I squeezed him tighter. I didn't want to let go. I didn't know if I'd ever see him again. I wish I'd had a vision of that, wished I knew this would turn out all right and everything would end up fine. But all I did know was that he wasn't going to die in the Gray.

I forced myself to let go and nudged him in the direction of the ring. He hurried across the clearing, quickly pressed a pattern, and stepped through the blinding white light.

The light slowly dissipated and I stared at the empty space, my heart aching and my stomach tight with uncertainty.

I was just about to step out of the underbrush and let the ring take me to the Black Tower, when I heard the creak of wagon wheels and the slow, rhythmic clomp of hooves on the hard-packed dirt road.

I ducked back behind the cover of the bushes and watched as a long procession of merchants and farmers, some with their carts full, some with their carts empty, come down the road. They were led by a middle-aged man with medium brown skin who wore a worn leather jerkin and a sheathed short sword at his hip — most likely a guardsman from the town — and an older man in a cream and gold robe — the town's priest.

Most merchants and those who regularly used the fae rings to travel knew the patterns to take them to where they wanted to go, but anyone who didn't travel frequently wouldn't know the correct pattern and would need the priest.

The procession was long, and I didn't want to walk

up to the ring and have it awaken without me touching it. Even if the merchants, farmers, and village people didn't know what the ring awakening without touching it meant, I was sure the priest of the Great Father would.

And while approaching the ring with everyone watching would be an opportunity to test my disguise as a boy, I didn't know what kind of reaction I'd get. I was a sacrifice, no longer really a person in Erellod. Would they shun me? Pity me?

Without a doubt they'd remember my red hair and I didn't want that, either. So I waited as everyone took their turn, either lighting up the pattern they already knew and stepping through or asking the priest to do it.

By the time the guardsman and the priest had headed back to town and stepped out of sight, the sun was setting with reds and oranges on the western horizon and velvety darkness was creeping from the east.

I took a quick moment to listen for anyone else, then hurried out of the underbrush to the ring, the fire in my arm bursting to life. I didn't want to risk another group approaching before I went through, and I didn't know if the rings were used all night long or not. If I didn't go now, I'd probably lose my nerve — at least until the binding spell forced me to go through a ring or it killed me.

White light blossomed in the ring before I was halfway across the clearing and fully filled the ring by the time I got there.

With a deep breath that did nothing to steady my nerves, I tightened my grip on my rucksack and strode through.

The ring's magic tingled over my body, and I walked into a cold mist that curled around me, chilling my skin.

I stood on a wide, bricked area with a road trailing ahead of me down a slope. Except I couldn't see past the circle of light blazing from the ring to see where the road led, and when the magic in the ring vanished, I was plunged into darkness. There wasn't a glimmer of sunset on the horizon, and only a hint of moonlight behind thick clouds to tell me which way was east.

I blinked, trying to get my eyes to adjust to the dim light. I could see a few paces ahead of me, but that was it, and there was no indication of where I should go or even that the Black Tower was anywhere near me.

Off in the distance something screeched and the cold wind gusted, swirling the mist around my legs and making me shiver.

I should have taken a second cloak when we'd fled Herstind, but Sawyer only had one and I hadn't wanted to take the time to go to my room to get mine. That, and my cloak wasn't practical like Sawyer's. It was red with gold embroidery along the hem and distinctly feminine.

The screech came again. Louder and closer and didn't sound like it had come from a bird.

Another screech and another, these ones lower in pitch. Then two more. All getting closer, coming from all around me.

My pulse lurched. There were monsters in the Gray. From their screams, it sounded like they'd found prey, and I had a horrible feeling that prey was me.

CHAPTER 11
Sage

I GLANCED BACK at the ring, a looming shadow in the darkness with no hint of the brilliant white magic that had filled it moments ago. I only knew the patterns for Olinon near Herstind castle and Addur, the capital, and Edred was sure to look for me at both of those places.

That, and I had no idea if the ring would let me awaken it now that I was in the Gray.

The screeching grew louder and I jerked my attention back to the road — or rather the mouth of the road because that was all I could see.

If this was the Black Tower's ring then the road had to lead to the tower. It wouldn't make sense to step out of the ring and then have to go around it to head to the Tower.

Another screech, this one high-pitched and long,

making my heart— No, my whole body freeze. At least one of the monsters was close.

I gritted my teeth and heaved against the fear freezing me in place. I wasn't going to go down trembling in front of the ring. I could at least try to get to safety. I had to run. Now.

I bolted down the road, praying it led toward the Black Tower and that the tower wasn't too far away. Most rings were near towns, some even inside them — although that was considered a risk since if an enemy managed to control another ring, they could march into the center of town past any defenses.

I hadn't expected the ring in the Gray to be within the Black Tower's defensive wall, but now I was afraid it was more than a couple hundred yards away. And with the barely-there moonlight and heavy mist, I'd have no way of knowing how close or far it was.

The frozen wind gusted, swirling the mist around me, revealing more of the road along with a shadow monster the size of a large, misshapen dog.

The monster was all black and stood on four legs. It had spikes sticking up from it in all directions, and a mouth full of teeth. Too many pointy teeth.

It threw its head back and screeched, the sound clawing down my spine.

A chorus of screeches answered from all around me and another monster, this one mottled white and gray like the mist, joined the first one on the road, blocking my way.

I jerked around to run back to the ring, but three more monsters stepped out of the mist, blocking my path. These were a mix of black and gray, just as big as the first one, and with far too many teeth as well.

My pulse roared in my ears, my heart pounding so hard I was afraid it would tear out of my chest. I had to fight. Even if I wanted to run — and I still had no idea which direction was the best choice — I was going to have to fight my way past them. Except I had a horrible feeling I wasn't going to be able to out-run them.

Which left me fighting all five of them to the death. Most likely my own.

I drew Sawyer's sword and widened my stance.

This wasn't the way things were supposed to go. But then I hadn't had a vision of what would happen to me when *I* stepped into the Gray, only what would happen to Sawyer.

I hadn't wanted to trade my life for his, but if that was what it came down to, then I would. Between us, he was the one who could protect the people of Herstind March from Edred. I was just a girl, who, once I was married off, would likely never step foot in Herstind again.

The first monster who'd blocked my way screeched again, and I spun around to face it.

It lunged at me and I heaved to the side.

Its wickedly long claws snagged in my rucksack, ripping it open. My clothes, ruined dress, and shoes tumbled out, and two of the monsters leaped on them. They screeched and snarled and tore into them with teeth and claws with a ferocity that filled me with terror.

That was going to be me.

I stumbled back, but the first monster swiped again, snagging its claws in my rucksack and yanking me toward it. I bent forward and twisted, slipping the rucksack's strap over my head and sacrificing it to the monster.

But the sudden loss of force that had been pulling me toward the monster made me stumble back and another creature screeched and leaped at me.

I sliced at it with my sword, cutting off one of its spikes and drawing a very dog-like snarl, then swung again, remembering to press my attack and not be shocked that I'd actually hit it.

But it swiped at me, forcing me to wrench out of the way, and I missed it completely.

Behind me, the other monsters screeched and snarled, the sound sharper than the sounds they'd been making while tearing apart my clothes.

They were going to attack again.

I spun to face them, wildly swinging my sword, hoping to hold them back. Somehow, I clipped the snout of one of them, but another one barreled into me and knocked me to the ground.

It slammed a heavy paw onto my already-bruised chest, sending agony shooting through my body and stealing my breath, and leaned close, snarling.

Black saliva dripped from its jaws onto my cheek so cold it felt like ice water, and my body shook with fear while my mind screamed at me to fight, get up, do something.

I heaved against its enormous weight but wasn't strong enough to move it.

Come on. Get up. Get up!

The other monsters drew close, screeching and snarling.

My breath grew shallow and ragged with terror.

Fight back! I screamed at myself and swung my sword.

But my arm was at the wrong angle to get in a good strike, certainly not anything that would get the monster off me, let alone kill it.

Shit!

Shit shit shit.

I bashed at it with the sword, barely doing any damage.

I was not going to die in the Gray.

I. Would. Not.

My free hand bumped the hilt of my dagger, and my thoughts lurched to something the armsmaster before Pylos had said while teaching me and Sawyer. Shorter blades were better in close combat. And this was as close as combat could get.

I yanked the dagger free and jammed it up into the monster's neck. Black blood, just as cold as the saliva, spurted over my face and chest.

The monster howled, staggered off me, and collapsed.

I didn't know if it was dead and I didn't have time to check.

I heaved to my knees, holding out both the sword and the dagger. I had almost no training fighting with a weapon in each hand, but I didn't want to drop — and likely lose — either weapon and didn't have time to sheath one of them. I barely had time to get to my knees before two other monsters lunged at me.

Time stuttered, slowing into a horrific frieze. I wasn't going to be able to fight off two monsters. I'd barely been able to fight off one. But I wasn't going to be able to get to my feet before they struck, and even if by a miracle I did, I still wasn't going to be able to run away.

I dove toward the one on my right, aiming my sword for its throat. If I was going to go down, I was going to take at least one of them with me or die trying.

The monster twisted and my blade skimmed its side, slicing off a few spikes, and I heaved out of its way.

But I was surrounded and any direction I went took me closer to another monster.

I tumbled toward a slightly smaller, mostly gray, monster.

It snarled and the muscles in its back legs bunched, readying to leap at me, just as an enormous black horse galloped out of the mist.

The rider leaned in his saddle and swung a sword longer and wider than mine and decapitated the monster in one powerful stroke.

I tried to rise and run to him, but the monster I'd missed, swiped at me, its claws catching in my jerkin, and wrenched me back to the ground. My head hit the bricked road and for a moment darkness overwhelmed the mist and screeching monsters.

Then another rider broke out of the mist, killing another monster with one swing, and the first rider grabbed the front of my sword belt, hauled me up, and slung me across the neck of his horse as if I were a sack of grain, sending more pain shooting through my chest.

"Fucking moron," the rider snarled, as the second rider turned and galloped back the way they'd come.

The first rider followed, one hand on my back pinning me to his horse, stomach-down, the other still holding his sword.

The two remaining monsters screeched and at least a dozen more cried back in response. More were coming. Their screeches drew closer, and I caught glimpses of them through the mist, racing alongside the horses. Large ones and smaller ones, some all black, some mottled, and some ghostly white.

"Open the gate," the rider in front yelled.

My bruised chest hurt, my body screamed in pain from being bounced against the horse while it galloped, and I couldn't catch my breath. The rider holding me didn't seem to care, and once we'd raced through a partially open gate into a wide bailey lit with torches, he shoved me off his horse.

I landed on my butt, the impact rattling up my spine and making my teeth snap together.

"Fucking moron," he snarled again. "Everyone knows you don't enter the Gray after sundown."

He glared at me, and his gaze locked with mine, his silver eyes freezing me in place and making my heart skip a beat.

He was fae. My second fae today, and while logically I knew I'd meet more fae since half of the Black Guard was fae, I was still stunned to be face to face with another one so soon.

CHAPTER 12
Sage

THE FAE who'd rescued me wasn't as beautiful as Lord Quill. His face was squarer, more rugged and rough, and he had three silvery white scars running across the bridge of his nose and halfway across his left cheek as if he hadn't been fast enough to get completely out of the way of one of those monster's claws. His gaze was hard, filled with a simmering anger, but there was still something breathtaking about him. Perhaps that was just because he was fae. The tales said all of his kind were mesmerizing and so far, I couldn't disagree.

His dark hair — it could have been brown or black, it was hard to tell in the flickering torchlight — had a streak of white or silver running from his left temple, the lack of color a shocking contrast to the rest of his hair. It was longer than Lord Quill's, but still only reached his shoulders and wasn't the long hair the tales all claimed fae had. He'd pulled half of it back in a topknot, exposing his long and delicately pointed ears, and he wore the same black leather armor as Lord Quill had. But instead of a sheath for his sword and two daggers, he had that and half a dozen more daggers of various lengths strapped to his body.

His gaze raked down me and I shivered in fear. Did he know I was a girl? Had I failed before I'd even started?

Then his eyes narrowed and I realized he was staring at my arm with the binding spell. Could all fae see the spell?

No, if they could Lord Quill would have known I'd taken Sawyer's place and would have stopped me before I'd gotten this far.

Which meant whoever this fae was, he could either control the spell or was important enough that he was able to see or sense it.

"And they're now sending me children, years away from shaving." He swung out of the saddle and handed the reins to a human man with sharp brown eyes and light brown skin the same shade as most of the people in Herstind March. He was probably only a few years older than me — my real age of twenty not Sawyer's fifteen — and he wore the same black armor as the fae who'd save me. "Congratulations, Vyell. Your evening stable shift has been cut in half for the rest of your rotation. This idiot here will take your first half of the shift after the evening meal."

"Yes, Lord Commander," Vyell said.

The fae, the Lord Commander of the Black Guard, turned his attention back to me. "You're also getting the full stable shift in the morning, too. Report to the stable at the second bell. You'll muck the stalls, day and night, until you're no longer stupid."

He turned and marched across the bailey toward an enormous building that towered wide, dark, and imposing, half shrouded in shadows and mist despite the many torches around us.

"Well lucky you," the other rider said to Vyell as he dismounted and handed over his reins. "A little extra lieu time."

The man, Vyell, flashed him a huge smile and led the horses off to a long one-story building that took up most of the left-hand side of the bailey, leaving me with just the other rider.

He was human as well with shaggy brown hair, brown eyes, a deep tan, and was older than me by probably ten or fifteen years. His face was hard, all sharp lines, and his jaw had a heavy dusting of dark stubble, making him look rougher than — although not as dangerous as — the Lord Commander. But there was also a softness to his gaze that the Lord Commander hadn't had.

His lips quirked and his gaze dipped down my

body, making me want to hug myself and hide. "I think you can put those away."

"I can what—?" I snapped my mouth shut and cleared my throat, my pulse leaping in a quick tattoo again. I needed to remember to lower my voice and speak gruffly. Not saying anything would probably be safest, but I doubted I'd be able to get away with that, especially if I was going to be in the Tower for more than a few days.

The man pulled a cloth from a pocket sewn into his jerkin and held it to me. "You should probably clean them first, though. Shadow blood is nasty stuff."

"Clean them—?" I asked as gruffly as I could. And jeez, why couldn't I get a full sentence out?

"Your weapons." He dipped his gaze down my body again and I realized he wasn't looking at me but my hands still clutching my sword and dagger as if my life depended on it.

I tucked my sword under my arm — since I didn't want to sheath it while covered in monster blood — took the offered cloth and wiped my dagger. He took another cloth and cleaned his own blade before sliding it home.

"So," he said as I sheathed my dagger and wiped my sword. "Are you arrogant to think you could use the ring after sunset or just stupid?"

So much for thinking that softness in his gaze said

he was less pissed off at me than the Lord Commander.

"Not *everyone* knows you shouldn't enter the Gray after sunset." And it had barely been sunset when I'd left. I hadn't expected full night when I'd stepped through the ring.

"So, you're a noble who never thought his name would be called." He jerked his chin and headed toward the monstrous building at the back of the bailey. "Well, you're not a lord now. You're a grunt like the rest of us and you'd be wise to learn that quickly."

"Yes, my lord," I mumbled, the submissiveness Edred had beaten into me over the last eight years kicking in on instinct, and I hunched my shoulders, trying to look smaller and less... well, less like me, because Edred never liked how I looked, and being smaller and nonconfrontational had saved me from a number of beatings.

"I'm not a lord. Only the Lord Commander and the captains of the Gold Tower, White Tower, and Shadow Guard are lords." He glanced at me, his eyes narrowing, and I realized I was acting like a woman and not a boy. Sawyer had always stood straight and met Edred's gaze even when the Marquis was yelling at him.

I forced myself to straighten and meet his gaze. "How should I address you?"

"Grefin."

"Just Grefin?" I asked, as we drew closer to the enormous building.

"Don't let it break your feeble mind, noble. The only things you learned in your old life that are useful are how well you swing your sword, how to shoot a bow, and how to fight from horseback," he said. "The Lord Commander doesn't care how well you can dance, which fork you're supposed to use, or if you know how to properly address a duke, a baron, or a princess."

We reached a wide set of steps leading up to a pair of massive doors that most likely opened to the great hall. The building was made of enormous stone blocks and towered four-stories high with thick crenellations at the top barely visible through the mist.

To my right was a squat building that didn't appear attached to the main building made of a strange semi-opaque material that could only be something made by the fae. It glowed a soft white, blending in with the mist around us, and I could see hints of strange shadows inside that thankfully didn't move.

Grefin headed left, away from the glowing building and the wide steps. He marched me to a part of the building that looked like it had sections jutting out from it — although it was hard to tell since there was less torchlight on this side of the structure. Light glowed between the cracks of dozens of shutters at random intervals. There were a few in a row, then nothing, then one or two more, but it suggested that all three stories were covered in windows.

"The quartermaster has already retired for the day and I'm not going to bother him just for you. You can get your gear after the midday meal with the rest of the novices."

"Yes, m—" I bit the inside of my cheek.

Grefin snorted. "You must have been last in line to show such deference to just about anyone."

Or I was a woman and was required to show deference to *everyone*.

He opened a door partially hidden in an alcove. Inside, illuminated by a lantern that glowed yellow like a flame but didn't flicker like one, was a narrow staircase curling up all three floors and down into a cellar, and another door leading into the rest of the building. "Well good news for you. Your birth order doesn't matter here. Prove your skill and even you can be given an elite assignment."

"Elite assignment?" I asked as he led us up the stairs.

"They didn't tell you anything. Or you didn't bother to learn." He stopped at the door at the top of the stairs and glared at me. "Lord Rider doesn't like lazy. Everyone pulls his own weight here, one way or another."

And that one way or another probably involved

being given the worst assignments, like mucking out the stalls.

I opened my mouth to argue with him, but snapped it shut. If they wanted to think I was lazy, I'd prove them wrong. If they wanted to think I was stupid, so be it. The whole point of being here was to go unnoticed until Sawyer was safe, and the more time that passed, the safer he'd be.

Grefin's eyes narrowed again, staring me down as if daring me to argue with him.

I fought to maintain eye contact, but it made my pulse race. Women didn't stare men down. They lowered their gaze and complied with whatever they were told.

"Definitely bottom of the pack," Grefin huffed, and he opened the door.

CHAPTER 13
Sage

INSIDE WERE MORE of the strange lanterns, their light dimmer than the light in the stairwell, and narrow wooden doors. Lots of doors. There was a door every few paces and they went all the way to the end of the hall on both sides.

Grefin strode down the hall to another one that bisected the first where a group of five human men who looked to be older than me but younger than Grefin and all in identical black leather armor lounged in a small seating area. The area consisted of a couch, four chairs, and small table, and their conversation fell silent as every eye landed on me and their gazes turned appraising.

I fought not to hunch my shoulders at their attention. They were all bigger than me, taller and broader. Two of them weren't wearing vambraces and had their shirtsleeves rolled up, revealing strong forearms that suggested the rest of them was muscular and well-developed from the rigors of being in the Black Guard.

No wonder the Lord Commander thought I was a child. Compared to these men, I was.

Grefin gave them a tight nod but kept walking. He turned left at the intersection, followed that hall to the end, took another left then finally stopped at a door beside a set of stairs that didn't have a door blocking it off.

"The first bell rings the morning meal. Easiest way to explain how to get there: follow everyone else." He opened the door, revealing a small room with a shuttered window at the back, a narrow cot along the wall with a trunk at the cot's foot, and a washbasin on a small stand with a strange metal handle close to the door so you could kneel on the trunk and use the basin. "This is your room."

"I have my own room?"

"Yeah." Grefin rolled his eyes at me.

Oh, thank the Great Father. Relief flooded me. I wasn't going to have to keep my secret while bunking with dozens of men in one room. It had been too late to change my mind once I'd taken Sawyer's binding spell, but I was terrified at the idea of being so vulnerable and knew I'd always be on my guard.

"I'm sure it's not as fancy as you're used to," Grefin

said, his voice dripped with sarcasm, "but we aren't a prison."

I shot him a dry look before I could stop myself and rubbed my wrist, still ever-so-slightly warm from the binding spell, then jerked my attention back to the room when I realized what I was doing.

"It's *not* a prison. This might not be the life you wanted, but it's not a punishment. Not everyone has enough to eat or a roof over his head like a noble. We work for it, but we get three meals, clean clothes, lessons in numbers and letters if we want it, a monthly stipend, and—" He stepped into the room and pressed his hand against a crystal embedded in the wall by the basin. Light flickered under his hand and grew brighter. "You get your own room."

"Why don't the people in the kingdoms know about this?" I asked, stepping into the room, staring at what could only be a magical fae light before turning my attention to the basin. There was something wrong with it. It looked like it was attached to the stand and it had a hole in the center.

"Some parts of the kingdom do know. Not all novices see themselves as sacrifices."

There was that idea again. It was similar to what Lord Quill had said, that some see it as an honor and a duty and were raised knowing they'd join the guard when they were old enough.

Grefin sighed and rolled his eyes at me. "That's a

pump." He pumped the handle up and down a few times until water spilled into the basin and disappeared down the hole.

"What—?" I jerked back to avoid the inevitable puddle on the stone floor, making Grefin throw his head back and laugh.

"Man, I love you novices! You always do that. Every time." He picked up a stopper that had been sitting on the stand beside the pump and set it in the hole in the wash basin then pumped in more water, filling the bowl halfway. "This place was built with fae magic so there's a pipe attached the basin and pipes throughout the Tower. There's a lot of hard work here, but lugging water around isn't one of them."

"Next you're going to tell me you have indoor privies like the palace in Addur or the Gold Tower," I huffed, except I couldn't see a chamber pot. But that only meant if I had to relieve myself, I'd have to leave the building and hike across the bailey to wherever the privy was.

"*And* there's also a whole fae bathhouse in the cellar, with cleaning and healing pools. Any set of stairs in the barracks will take you to it." He gave me a pointed look. "You probably don't want to sleep covered in shadow blood. You only get clean sheets every two rotations."

I glanced down at the black blood covering my

jerkin, shirtsleeves, and hands, and could feel it, sticky and itchy on my face and neck.

Grefin stepped out of the room and grabbed the doorlatch. "Don't forget where your room is and don't forget to stay in the great hall after the midday meal to be assessed with all the other novices. The stable-master will expect you in the stables by the second bell. That means it'll ring twice after the first ring. The first bell is at dawn. If you don't waste time, you can bathe and eat your morning meal before the second bell."

He shut the door, leaving me in my tiny room. I stood there, listening to his footsteps get farther away, my mind whirling. Except I couldn't make myself focus.

I was in the Black Tower.

No one had yelled at me for being a girl and this was now my life for as long as I could keep my secret. Sawyer's life depended on me.

I really hoped he was all right, that he'd managed to get through the ring and was on his way to the border.

My gaze dipped to my hands and the black blood covering them.

I'd almost been killed.

Fear squeezed around my heart and my hands started to shake. If the Lord Commander and Grefin hadn't rescued me, I would have been torn to shreds like my clothes and rucksack.

I needed to get smarter and stronger. Fast.

I *was* going to survive the Gray. Whatever it took. And then I was going to get Sawyer's rightful title back. Even if Edred could escape the king's justice, he wouldn't escape mine, not for what he'd done to Sawyer and our mother.

I gritted my teeth, squared my shoulders, and reached to dip my hands into the water still in the basin.

Except I didn't have anything to dry myself with... and I no longer had a second shirt or pair of pants. Which meant I was going to have to venture down to the bathhouse if I wanted to wash up.

If the Tower's bathhouse was anything like the tales, there'd be towels and different soaps and all manner of beautiful, naked fae women wandering around.

Heat seared my cheeks.

I knew there wouldn't be naked fae woman tending the baths since this was the Black Tower and there were no women here — although maybe there were since Grefin had seemed so pleased to mention it — but without a doubt there would be naked men.

Lots of naked men.

And while I'd caught glimpses of a few naked men before, Edred had been strict to the point of severe punishment that my maidenhood remained intact. I'd fetch a better bride price if I was still a virgin and no one wanted to risk his ire, not even to give me a glimpse of my inevitable future.

Although what Edred didn't know, was that I wasn't a virgin anymore. I'd had an encounter with a boy I'd grown up with behind the stables when I'd become old enough for Edred to send me to my first arranged husband — before said husband had died and I'd been given to his son, who thankfully had been lost at sea before I could be sent to him. Edred had taken everything from me: my mother, my freedom, and my happiness, and I wasn't going to let him take my very first time with a man, too.

But it had been dark, neither of us had completely undressed, and it had been over shortly after if had started.

And really, if that was what sex was like, I was fine remaining chaste. Clearly the minstrels exaggerated it. It wasn't breathtaking and romantic, and since a woman married whomever her father told her to, there wouldn't ever be any professions of love for me.

I sucked in a steadying breath. Yes, the two fae men I'd seen had been shockingly beautiful and had captured my attention in ways it had never been captured before, but I could ignore them and the other fae here, even if they were fully naked.

And I wasn't going to think about what sex with them would be like—

Nope. Not going to think about that at all.

Besides, I didn't have to stay long in the bathhouse and fight my embarrassment. I just needed to be there long enough to grab a couple of towels and hopefully a bar of soap and return to my room. Having the pump and basin was an unexpected, wonderful blessing. I hadn't known how I was going to bathe and keep my secret. I hadn't thought that far ahead. But now I could wash myself in my room and not have to worry about sneaking down to the baths in the middle of the night.

I might just be able to do this... at least long enough for Sawyer to get away.

CHAPTER 14

Sage

MY NERVES STEELED against seeing more of the men of the Black Tower than I really wanted, I slipped out of my room and down the stairs just outside my door.

Grefin had said any of the stairs in the barracks would take me to the bathhouse and the stairs closest to my door meant I wouldn't have to try to look masculine while walking past that group of men who'd stared at me before — although I now realized they'd been staring at me in part because I looked like a child but also because I was covered in shadow monster blood.

The stairs ended in a plain wooden door like all the other doors I'd encountered in the barracks, and I cracked it open to peek first so I'd be prepared for what lay inside. But the only thing on the other side of the door was another stone hall that stretched ahead and to my right and was brightly lit by more fae lanterns.

Heat and moisture filled the air, indicating that there was hot water nearby, and I stepped into their embrace, savoring how much it was like the Herstind I loved and had left. Ahead, there were a few doors, but only on one side of the hall, as if I stood on an outside edge and the hall traveled the perimeter of the bathhouse. Other than that, there was nothing to indicate what lay behind each door.

In search of something to tell me where I was going, I headed right. At the end of the hall was another door at the corner leading to a stairwell and more hall stretching to the left that looked identical to the hall I'd just walked down: long, stone, brightly lit, and with a few unmarked, wooden doors.

That hall turned left to another hall and another, and I was back where I'd started. I hadn't run into anyone, so I hadn't been able to ask directions, and each door had been identical. Even the stairwells had been the same, and I'd really hoped one of them would have been bigger indicating a main entrance. Which meant I was going to have to open a door at random and hope for the best.

I looked at the two doors closest to me.

If I was setting up a bathhouse, I'd set towels just inside the door of every pool. Which meant all I'd need to do was open one, pop in, grab a towel, and leave. Maybe no one would notice me.

Maybe no one would be in the room?

Except I didn't even know if there were rooms on the other side. Maybe it was one big open area.

Shadows!

All right, if I was going to put the sacrifices anywhere, I'd put them in rooms the farthest away from anything useful and that included the baths. Which meant the door closest to me was probably a storage closet or a servant's entrance... not that they had servants in the Tower but—

Just pick a door!

I grabbed the latch for the closest door and eased it open a crack. Steam billowed in my face, blinding me for a moment, but once it cleared all I could see was a gold and white tiled corner and no towels. Not even a rack or a bench.

Swell.

I pushed the door open wider to search the room, and my gaze landed on the most stunning fae I'd seen so far.

He lounged in a pool large enough for two dozen people with steam curling from the water and caressing his skin. He was exactly like the fae from the tales with long white hair that surely reached his waist when he stood. Four thin braids at his temples held it back from his face and exposed his delicately pointed ears, while the rest was splayed across the tiles behind him, and a gold earring, adorned with tiny pearls, capped the tip of one ear and looped through three holes pierced down the side, catching the light.

He'd hooked his arms over the edge of the pool behind him, his muscles sculpted to perfection, and the water lapped halfway up his chest, giving a tantalizing glimpse of his muscular torso.

Then he looked at me, capturing me with eyes that were soft mesmerizing swirls of white, pink, purple, blue, and gold, and my whole essence stuttered, trapped within the whirlpool in his gaze.

"Ah, so you're the reason Rider's in a foul mood," he said, his words sliding through me, sending a shiver of sudden, shocking need thrumming low within me. "Why would you risk going through the ring after dark?"

"It wasn't fully dark when I stepped through," I said, barely managing to remember to sound gruff.

"You're that eager to become a novice? That's unusual for a human." He sat up, showing more of his chiseled chest, and my mind jumped to the fact that he was in a pool and had to be naked.

My essence stuttered again and I fought to think straight.

"Why do you call us that?" I blurted out, saying the first thing I could think of. "Grefin called me that, too. I'm a sacrifice." In a literal sense. Edred had purposefully ensured Sawyer's name would be called and I'd given up my freedom, possibly even my life, to save him.

"Because sacrifices have nothing to live for and that makes a man reckless. Reckless men get their fellow guards killed." His eyes narrowed. "But maybe that's why you stepped through the ring after dark. You're probably one of the youngest novices the humans have ever sent us. Maybe you'd rather the shadows deal with you than face the rest of your life in the Guard."

"It wasn't dark when I stepped through," I insisted.

Oh, shit.

I snapped my mouth shut. I shouldn't have talked back. Even if I was supposed to be a boy and could look him in the eyes — which were seriously distracting — I should have just bowed and agreed. He was still a fae which meant he was more powerful than me in every way.

"I didn't realize the sun set sooner in the Gray, my lord," I said, heaving my gaze to my feet.

"It seems your education has been lacking."

"Yes, my lord," I replied.

The sound of sloshing water taunted me to look up, telling me he was swimming closer, but I kept my gaze locked on my feet.

"And it seems I need to start right now," he said with a huff.

My breath picked up and I fought to stay where I was.

Edred had been a general in the king's army and he liked to *teach* lessons, too. It made sense that the Black Guard followed a similar discipline, especially since the members hadn't volunteered. The Lord Commander had already assigned me smelly labor, I should have expected a thrashing as well so I wouldn't forget what I learned.

"The first lesson is don't look at your feet," he said.

What?

My attention jerked up in surprise before I could stop it and I fell into his swirling eyes again. He'd shifted in the pool to lean his chest against the edge closest to me, his long hair trailing in the water behind him, undulating in the waves and showing me teasing flashes of his back and butt.

"You're a member of the Black Guard, you bow to no one. Not to me, the Lord Commander, my peoples' high priestess, or even your king. We're the guard against the shadows and we're always vigilant."

"Yes, my lord."

"Lesson number two," he continued. "Only the commander and the captains are called lord. Everyone else is just who they are."

"Grefin already explained that one," I murmured.

"And yet you're still showing me deference," he said, his lips curling into an enigmatic smile, and I couldn't tell if he was pleased that I wasn't following the 'no lord' rule or not.

Then he stood and my heart stopped. The water

sluiced over muscles honed to perfection and lapped around his hips, the churning water obscuring his cock. But as soon as the water stilled—

I heaved my attention up before I got an eye-full of something I feared would taunt me for the rest of my life and strained to keep my expression neutral. Except neutral was impossible so I twisted it from shock to hopefully gruff concern.

"For all I know you're one of the captains," I forced out, my mind screaming, caught between the urge to look and the need to get out of there before I revealed I was a girl.

He chuckled and climbed out of the pool.

Oh Father, save me!

CHAPTER 15
Sage

"You've got me there. I'm Talon, Captain of the Gold Tower, but I'd rather you drop the lord thing. Welcome to the Black Guard, novice." He held out his hand in the customary human men's greeting between equals of clasping forearms. Still completely naked!

I will not look. I will not look. I—

I raised my hand to complete the greeting and caught a glimpse of darkness. That drew my gaze down to my shadow-blood-covered hands and then past to his cock. It was at ease, but still bigger than I'd seen before... not that I'd gotten a very good look at many other cocks... but still. Of course, he was taller and broader than most of the men I knew, and certainly bigger than the boy I'd given my virginity to, so it would make sense he'd be bigger *there,* too. And now my thoughts were rambling.

"I ah…" I jerked my hand back. "I don't mean any offense, my lord, but I'm— My hands are— I'm sorry."

I was still staring at him, at his sculpted abs and muscular thighs, and his cock. Oh, Great Father, I was stuck. I had to look away. Now. Please. Look away!

Heat burned my face, and I knew that under the shadow blood splatter it was the same color as my hair.

"Ah— No." He grabbed a towel from a shelf beside me that I hadn't noticed — because I'd been staring at him — and quickly wrapped it around his hips. "It's me who should apologize. Most of the humans in the guard aren't fae-touched and my nudity isn't an issue."

"What—?" None of that made sense. Did he know about my strange premonitions?

But then realization kicked in. When a human was referred to as fae-touched it meant two possible things and both were said with disgust. The first was that he or she had a hint of magic and somewhere in their family someone had been cursed by a powerful fae.

The second was a man who was attracted to other men instead of women. All of the fae living in the Gold Tower in Erellod's capital were men and it was well known that they had intimate relationships with each other. I'd even heard from the most recent minstrel who'd visited Herstind castle that some of the fae in the Gold Tower had taken marriage vows with each other.

Lord Talon thought I was attracted to men.

"My magic heightens an attraction that's already there. It's most powerful on humans. If I'd know, I would have been more discreet." He paused, as if waiting for me to respond, but I couldn't think past the knowledge that Talon thought I was fae-touched to come up with a response.

"I won't say anything, if that's what you're worried about," he added. "You can keep it a secret, but you'll find the only ones who might give you trouble about it are novice humans. We have a few bonded mates among our fae guardsmen, and everyone learns pretty quickly what is and isn't acceptable behavior toward them."

"I—" I had no idea what to say about that. A part of me wanted to deny it. But if everyone thought I was attracted to men, I wouldn't have to fight so hard to hide it and it would explain why I was shy around everyone when they were naked.

"You'll still have to deal with the communal bathing rooms unless you can get an elite assignment. But your reaction won't be nearly as obvious if I'm not naked. Now come on," he said, picking up a black shirt that was a part of a heap of black clothing on the rack where the towel had been. "I'll show you to the towel room and a pool where you can clean up."

He turned his back on me and opened up the towel — likely to put on his pants — and my pulse stuttered.

I jerked away from him before I ended up staring at his butt.

"So, this is an elite pool?" I squeaked, unable to keep my voice gruff, the image of what his tight-muscled rear would look like jumping into my mind.

"No," he chuckled. "And it's safe to turn around now."

I turned as he drew closer and reached for the doorlatch. My pulse jerked and my face burned hotter. Even dressed in a black shirt, pants, and boots, he was stunning. And now I knew what lay under those clothes.

I had no idea how I was going to function, let alone pretend I was a guy, if I reacted like this with all the fae.

"Elite teams have a private bathing room in their suites for cleaning up." He opened the door and led me down to the other door.

I was going to smack myself if the towels were just behind that door. Of course, if I had picked the other door, then I wouldn't have gotten an eye-full of Talon... and I couldn't decide if that was a good thing or not.

"That's a soaking pool with healing water." He opened the door and led me into another hall with white, blue, and green tiles covering the ceiling, walls, and floor. It had a mix of wooden doors and open arch-ways and ended in a large wide arch, tiled with a gold and black pattern. "It's good for aches and bruises. Anyone can use it if they have the free time. Training only happens in the morning and afternoon so there usually isn't anyone down here this late after the evening meal. This is when I use the pool so my magic doesn't end up making someone uncomfortable."

We walked to the large arch. Inside was an enormous, thankfully empty, pool. Wisps of steam swirled above its surface, indicating it was still hot, but not as hot as the healing pool. At the back were a series of open stalls with buckets hanging overhead.

"Come back to this pool area. Leave your towel and clothes on the rack." He pointed to a large, five-shelf rack just inside the archway with a couple sets of clothes and towels. "Scrub the blood off in the rain stall then soak for a bit in the pool." He turned and headed deeper into the bathhouse, passing another arch with a smaller pool, before opening a wood door beside the large arch at the end. "This is the towel room. Clean towels on the rack. Dirty towels in the bin or in the laundry bin near your room."

"Laundry bin?"

"There are a couple on every floor in the barracks."

Of course there were. There was a bathhouse in the basement, a room for each guardsman, and water from a pump in every room. Why not a bin for laundry? Next, he was going to tell me we ate fresh vegetables in the winter as if we were all royalty.

"Everything will be explained when the other novices arrive tomorrow. For now, clean up and get a good night's sleep." He turned, strode to the end of the hall, and left.

I stared at the closed door.

The Black Tower wasn't at all what I'd expected.

The image of Talon's stunning naked body flashed through my mind's eye and my face burned again with embarrassment.

The fae, however, were so much more than I imagined.

They were just as seductive and alluring as I'd been warned against, and I was going to have to be very, very careful. Especially if they were as kind as Talon. Even if I'd been flustered at seeing him naked, he'd made me feel comfortable, that my life was safe with him.

And that was a dangerous feeling. I might be safe with him when we were fighting side-by-side as guardsmen, but I wouldn't be safe if he found out I was a girl.

CHAPTER 16
Sage

THE TOWEL ROOM had two sizes of white towels: big and small, and a small crate with various-sized bars of soap that — of course, because nothing at the Black Tower was what I'd expected — had a smell that reminded me of the forest instead of the ash and animal fat and cloying perfume I was used to.

I grabbed a couple bars of soap, a few small towels and a big one then hurried back up to my room, thankfully not running into anyone and having to explain why I'd come from the bathhouse still covered in shadow blood and holding a bundle of towels.

My door didn't have a bolt on the inside so I couldn't stop anyone from entering if I wanted to, but I still had to strip to clean myself and my clothes.

I prayed no one would just walk in as I shrugged out of my jerkin and shirt and unbound my chest. It was a relief to finally take a full deep breath after being bound for half a day, but unnerving to see the bruise Edred had given me. I was free from him now, hopefully forever, but I wasn't foolish enough to think my days of being bruised were at an end.

I scrubbed away the blood from my face, neck, hands, and forearms, then washed my shirt and jerkin as best I could since I didn't have anything else to wear and I wasn't going to put on blood-encrusted clothes in the morning, even if I was just going to muck out the stables.

With my clothes clean and draped over the basin and pump so they could dry, and the fae light as dim as I could make it — which was nearly out save for a pinprick of light in its center — I collapsed onto the cot, pulled the blanket over me, and closed my eyes.

Except despite my exhaustion, I couldn't get my mind to stop spinning.

Edred had manipulated the lottery and Sawyer wasn't safe until he was out of the Five Great Kingdoms. The rings closest to any of the borders, even in Helialonde and Thermalea were still at least a month of travel away by horseback, and there was a chance Sawyer would have to sell the horse to survive. Although hopefully he'd have enough common sense to sell my pendant first.

Then my thoughts flitted to the monsters in the Gray and the Lord Commander calling me a moron.

I was going to have to keep my head down and not draw anymore attention to myself, and that meant not complaining about mucking the stable or whatever else the Lord Commander saw fit to punish me with.

But the thought of punishment made my mind leap to that strange moment with Talon and that made me think of his breathtaking body.

I didn't think I'd ever be able to look at him and not remember all that muscle... not to mention his cock. Would sex with him be as quick and unsatisfying as it had been with Royston?

That would be a serious disappointment.

Except that wasn't something I was going to find out... not that he'd be interested in me—

Which was also a disappointing thought and — *jeez!* — not something I should be thinking about.

I tried to shove the thoughts aside and prayed I'd just fall asleep, but my mind kept whirling around and around, always coming back to the image of Talon's naked body, water trailing over the hardened ridges of his abs, drawing my gaze back to—

This was ridiculous!

I jerked up and—

I wasn't in bed.

My pulse stuttered as my mind lurched, trying to figure out what had happened.

I sat on a patch of short, soft grass at the edge of a pool. Beyond lay a garden filled with flowers, their colors muted in the dim torchlight and pale moonlight, and a stone path leading from the pool to a courtyard outside of a towering building... or was that a tree?

It sort of looked like both, but I couldn't exactly tell with the night's shadows partially obscuring it.

Tall pillars shaped like beautiful women held up a gauzy, green canopy over the courtyard, and more of the cloth draped between them. A gentle breeze made the cloth billow and caress around the statues' legs like dresses, giving me glimpses of the people inside— No, from their tall, graceful figures they were *fae*.

I had to be dreaming. I'd been thinking about how beautiful Talon was and drifted into the most beautiful dream. That, and it was the only explanation how I'd ended up in a garden when I'd gone to bed in my room in the Black Tower, and how I now wore a red dress when I'd been naked. Not to mention how my head felt heavy, like my hair was long again and my chest didn't hurt nearly as badly as it had when I'd gone to sleep.

I stood — my feet still bare — and took in the dress. It looked like it was made half from the same strange, gauzy material curtaining the courtyard, and half with exquisite lace depicting a flowering vine that curled from the hem at my toes, up one side, and wrapped around my hips and bodice, hiding just enough of me to not be indecent. The bodice was cut low, in a style from the Southern Isles, and accentuated the inside curve of my small breasts and clung around my ribcage before flaring out around my hips into a full floor-length skirt.

The breeze fluttered my skirt around my legs, and I stepped closer to the pool to use it as a mirror and get a better look at myself.

But a part of me couldn't believe what I was seeing, and I stared at my reflection, stunned for a long moment.

I was beautiful.

I'd never been so beautiful before, only proving this was a dream.

My eyes were a vibrant green, like the emerald in the pendant I'd given to Sawyer and not their usual brown, and my hair was a darker, more vibrant red than my usual color. It hung half loose, reaching my waist, and half piled on my head in an intricate plaited style that turned my sharp features into stunning sculpted lines and drew my gaze to my delicately pointed ears.

Strange red spots on my skin encircled my neck like a necklace, trailed between my breasts, and disappeared beneath the bodice of my dress. The spots were of varying shapes and sizes, although none were bigger than my thumbnail, and were oddly clustered, some close together, some farther apart in no discernable pattern.

I brushed a finger over them. They pulsed with a soft, red glow and warmed against my skin. A heat fluttered in my chest for a moment, then the heat and light vanished and I was back to myself... or as myself as I was going to get in this strange dream.

"My lady, are you strolling alone?" a sensual masculine voice purred and the reflection of a fae stepped into sight beside mine.

I raised my gaze to look at him properly. He was beautiful like all the fae I'd already seen but didn't have the same magnetic pull Lord Quill or Talon had. He was taller than me and as broad-shouldered as the Lord Commander had been, and his waist-length black hair had been braided back at his temple and hung loose down his back like Lord Talon's, showing off the gold earrings on each ear tip. His eyes were so dark they appeared black in the pale moonlight, and he studied me with an intensity that sent a shiver of uncertainty sliding through me.

His lips curled back in a smile that only made me more nervous. He looked... hungry and not in the sense of needing food, but of wanting me. Some of Edred's men had also looked at me that way and while this fae was better at hiding it than Edred's men, I could still see it and it still made my stomach churn with worry.

"Have you gotten anything to eat yet?" he asked as he gestured to a bench on the other side of the pool. "Why don't you take a seat and I'll bring you something."

"Planning on keeping the new arrival to yourself?" another masculine voice asked behind me.

I spun around to face another fae, just as stunning as the first but with white hair, pale yellow eyes, and warm brown skin. Beside him was another man, a mix between the two with gold hair — cut short unlike the other two — and dark eyes.

"She looked hungry," the first man replied.

"And more than capable of walking," White Hair shot back. "Come." He held out his arm for me to take. "Everyone will want to meet the new arrival."

"I... ah..." I glanced into White Hair's eyes and caught a glimpse of the same hunger Black Hair had.

Maybe this was my inner most desire: to be craved by beautiful men, especially since acting like a boy and chopping off my hair made me even less desirable than before. Maybe seeing Talon naked had awakened something in me that I'd been suppressing because no matter what I'd wanted, I'd never be able to have it.

Up until I'd made the reckless decision to take Sawyer's binding spell, my body hadn't been my own. I might have been able to have more sexual encounters if I'd wanted to, at least until I was sent to my husband, but I would have always ended up with a man of Edred's choosing.

White Hair didn't wait for a response. He captured my hand, hooked it into the crook of his arm, and led me up the path to the courtyard. The third fae who'd yet to speak, Short Hair, pulled aside one of the gauzy curtains and White Hair ushered me inside.

A hush fell over the courtyard. I hadn't even realized people had been talking.

Of course, it was a dream, there might not have been anyone talking for it to suddenly feel as if a silence had descended around me.

The courtyard, illuminated by hundreds of tiny lanterns all with the steady glow of the fae lights was large and stretched into the tree-building. And it was indeed half building and half tree with a strange mix of stone walls and tree trunks and branches. Conversation areas of benches and couches and chairs, some stone, some with plump, plush cushions, were scattered throughout the area along with tables with food and drink.

There were at least a hundred fae men in the courtyard, all beautiful and bigger than most humans. They sat, stood, gathered in groups for conversation, or at the food and drink tables about to pour wine or fill a plate of food, and all of them had stopped whatever they were doing and stared at me.

"A new arrival," someone murmured.

"Look at her marks."

"—not yet mated."

"—talk to her. You might be one—"

"Something to eat, my lady?" White Hair asked.

"She's probably thirsty," Black Hair replied, not giving me a chance to speak.

"Come stroll with me," another man said, drawing close, towering over me.

"No me," said a third — or was that a fourth?

"We can go together," another man offered.

At least two dozen of them crowded close, all eager, all bigger than me, forcing me to look up at them and making me feel small and helpless. Some of them looked hungry like Black Hair and White Hair, others looked eager, while a few looked... hopeful? The three men who wanted to stroll with me glanced at each other and something passed between them.

"We'll show you the garden," the first guy said, as he drew closer, his hand outstretched in an offer for me to take it.

"No," Black Hair snapped, possessively grabbing my arm. "She's just arrived."

"Then she should be shown around so she doesn't get lost," the first guy shot back, taking another step toward me.

I shifted back, trying to put space between me and the men, but they moved with me, keeping close. Offers to sit, to eat, to stroll, to listen to music, to bathe were thrown out, each suggestion louder than the next as every man tried to be heard over the others.

Their voices roared around me and my pulse raced.

They were too close. They kept bumping into me. They were going to grab me and rip me apart.

Great Father, this wasn't a dream. It was a nightmare, a reminder that I was now surrounded by men in the Black Tower and didn't want them to know who I really was. And while the men in my dream were all vying for my attention, I doubted the men at the Tower would be so welcoming.

They crowded so close I could barely see the gauzy canopy above me, and my breathing turned sharp. I couldn't breathe. The world jostled and my thoughts spun. I needed space. I had to get out of there.

Leave me alone. Please. Stop touching me.

But I couldn't get the words out. I'd be punished if I made such demands. I'd be punished too if I fled, but I had to do something, and fleeing was safer than speaking up.

There was a space behind me. If I was fast enough, I could run through and find a way back to the garden. There was a chance if I ran away, my dream would make them chase me, but I couldn't keep standing there.

I jerked around and twisted sideways to bolt through the space between two of the men. Black Hair said something, but I ignored him and wrenched out of the way of another man. I bumped into someone, jerked away before he could grab me, caught a glimpse of gauzy green fabric, and raced toward it.

The window billowed the fabric across my path, but I shoved it aside, ran between two of the statues, and slammed face-first into something hard and black.

My world lurched, the impact stunning me, and with a yelp, I stumbled back and lost my balance. But before I could fall, a hand snapped out, grabbed my upper arm, and jerked me upright. He — and from his size and build he had to be a he — tugged me to his side and wrapped his arm around my waist, steadying me against him.

"What—" he snarled, the voice shockingly familiar.

That sounded like—

I jerked my gaze up and looked into the silver eyes of the Lord Commander of the Black Guard.

Oh, shit.

CHAPTER 17

Sage

I INWARDLY GROANED. It was going to be one of *those* dreams. The Lord Commander already thought I was an idiot and was already angry at me. My dream had to be feeding on my fear that when I woke, mucking the stables wasn't the only punishment he was going to give me.

"Find something else to do," he snarled.

Except he wasn't looking at me. He was glaring at the other men.

"But she's new," Black Hair said as the other men crowded behind him. "She needs someone to show her around."

"And if she wants you to show her around, she'll ask you." The Lord Commander's lips curled back, and he snarled, a lot like the shadow monsters had snarled.

I tried to slip from his grip, hoping he'd be too

upset with the others to notice — because hey, it was a dream and people could get away with things like that in dreams — but he didn't release me.

"You're here because you're no longer children," he said. "Stop acting like ones."

Black Hair glared back at the Lord Commander then jerked around. He gave White Hair and Short Hair a quick look, then pushed through the crowd and headed back into the courtyard, the other two following him.

The rest of the crowd grumbled and whispered and gave the Lord Commander dirty looks, but they all retreated, leaving me alone with him.

"Are you all right?" he asked, looking down at me with his strange, silver eyes.

Something powerful and breathtaking zinged through me, stealing my breath and making my thoughts stutter, but it was gone before I could figure out what it was or what it meant.

His grip on my upper arm tightened, steadying me, as he stepped back, his gaze searching mine... for what? I had no idea. "Are you all right?"

I nodded and fought to regain my mental balance. I wasn't even sure what my mind had tripped over. But to figure that out, I needed to look away.

Except just like with Lord Quill, I couldn't. My gaze slid down his body of its own volition, taking him in.

He looked exactly like he had when I'd seen him in

the Black Tower's bailey. My dream hadn't softened his features or hardened them. His dark hair — and the light was still too dim for me to tell if it was dark brown or black — was still half tied back in a topknot, the three scars still ran over his nose and across his cheek, and he still wore his black leather armor.

Only two things weren't the same: he wasn't bristling with weapons, and the look in his eyes was kinder, warmer, as if he didn't think I was a fool and hadn't unnecessarily risked his and Grefin's lives by stepping through the ring after dark. I wasn't just a child that had been thrust onto him, I was a woman who'd needed rescuing.

And I guess that was my mind telling me that as much as I wanted to be strong, that wasn't all I wanted to be. I'd made a reckless decision that had — most likely — permanently changed the course of my life. A life that could end up being very short if I made another foolish mistake in the Gray or someone found out my secret.

I'd had to be strong for years against Edred, trying to be obedient and unnoticed, but unable to stop myself when he hurt my brother. If I could have just let it go, I wouldn't have been beaten so often. But I hadn't been able to just stand there and watch. Just like I hadn't been able to let Sawyer be bound to the Black Tower when I knew he'd die.

And I had to keep being strong, because everything

was only going to get harder and more lonely. It wasn't safe to let anyone get close and there wasn't anyone I could turn to for help. Which was why my dream was turning the Lord Commander of the Black Guard, someone who I knew didn't like me, into an ally.

At least it was better than having him snap at me in my dreams, too.

"Some of the younger men still need to learn patience," he said. "I'm Rider."

I stared at him. Not Lord Commander or Lord Rider. Just Rider.

Of course, I'd dreamt myself into being a fae, which meant I was his equal… or as equal as a fae woman got, so why not just-plain-Rider? I didn't know much about fae culture or etiquette, but it seemed in this dream that I didn't have to be subservient to him. Guess that came from Talon's strange lecture about never looking down and only showing deference to the captains and Lord Commander of the Guard.

"Ah," he said, his voice gruff, his attention jumping past my shoulder. "Just the person to show you around."

I turned to see who he meant as a stunning fae woman with silver spots circling her neck and trailing over her collar bone like a necklace saw us and started heading our way. She was just as breathtaking as all the other fae I'd seen. More so, since she was a woman, something very few humans had actually seen. She wore a black dress made from a similar material as gauzy as mine that fluttered behind her when she walked, and her hair was dark like Lord Rider's—

No. Just Rider.

"I must be seeing things," she said, her voice sweet and soft and edged with a laugh. "Are you actually in the Garden talking to a woman?"

"Not intentionally," he huffed, making her laugh in full which made him scowl.

"Pardon my brother," she chuckled, sliding her attention to me. "I'm not even sure he knows what the word courting means."

"You know very well I'm not here to find a mate—"

"Which is why it's so shocking to see you in the company of a woman," she interrupted. "I'm Lark."

"Sage," I replied without thinking.

"Yes, well." He rolled his eyes at his sister. "The *children* haven't learned what courting means, either. She's new and still looks stunned from manifesting. I'm guessing it's your first time," he asked me.

"My first—" Manifesting? This dream was getting stranger and stranger.

"I'm here for a meeting," he added without waiting for my response and turned his attention back to Lark. "I can't wait until she gets her bearings and remembers how to put those children in their place. Can you show her around?"

"Any other day," she said. "But the priestess is

blessing the pool and all of my mates are here, not just manifesting." She pressed her hands to her belly in a way I'd seen many pregnant women do. "Tonight's the night. I just know it."

Something dark flickered in Rider's eyes so quickly I was sure I'd only noticed it because this was my dream. Then it vanished as he offered her a warm smile. "It will be."

"I'm sorry I can't show you the Garden," Lark said to me. "But I have no doubt I'll see you again and then I can show you all the little nooks just for us women that the men know nothing about."

She gave me a warm, welcoming smile, something I hadn't seen from another woman — hell, from anyone but Sawyer — for a long time, then turned to Rider and pulled him into a quick embrace. With another smile and a wave, she hurried along the outside edge of the courtyard to an archway leading into the tree-building where four fae men were waiting for her.

"Your sister is lovely," I said.

I didn't know why my dream had created her — I doubted the Lord Commander of the Black Guard even had a sister — but I wasn't going to question it or look too closely at it. Looking too closely usually changed the dream, twisting whatever was wonderful into something horrible. And my wonderful moments were going to be few and far between from now on. I'd take whatever I could get, even if it wasn't real.

"She was stunned her first time manifesting as well," he said, watching her and the men walk out of sight. "So dizzy she couldn't even stand. It happens to so few of us that some of the younger men, in their enthusiasm, forget it's possible. But—"

"Really, Rider?" a dry masculine voice asked behind me, so familiar it made my pulse leap. "Now's not the time to change your mind about mating."

I turned as Talon approached us. He was dressed in a two-toned gold jerkin that enhanced the golden shimmer in his mesmerizing, multi-colored eyes. He looked just as breathtaking as before, and, much as I feared, I couldn't help but think about him naked.

Heat flooded my face, and despite the fact that he glowered at me — a complete change of personality from when I'd walked in on him in the bathhouse — a soft ache blossomed low within me.

I bit back a huff of frustration. This dream was turning cruel. The one person who'd been nice to me at the Tower now looked at me with disgust. Of course, maybe this was my mind's way of reminding me that no matter how nice Lord Talon had been, I still had to watch everything I did and said.

Beside him, much to my surprise, with an apologetic half-smile, was Lord Quill, the fae who'd delivered the death sentence to my brother. He didn't wear the Guard's black armor either and instead wore a green jerkin that matched his emerald eyes, eyes that looked a lot like mine now.

"I haven't changed my mind about mating," he growled back. "She's new and disoriented from manifesting."

"And you're so chivalrous you're showing her around," Lord Talon replied, his tone dripping with sarcasm and drawing my gaze back to him. "We don't have time for this. Send her on her way."

"She's standing right here," Lord Quill said, and my attention, my whole essence jumped to him. "Pardon my companion." He shot Lord Talon a withering glare. "Our meeting is important, but I'm sure Rider will look for you when we're done."

"No," Rider snapped, making my essence jerked back to him as if just by speaking these men has a strange possession over my body. "You've figured yourself out?"

My thoughts stalled on his mouth. He'd said something. But his demeanor had changed from welcoming to brusque.

I took a step back, his sudden change of emotion shocking me, despite knowing this was a dream.

"Have you figured yourself out?" Talon repeated, making my essence snap back to him. He wanted me gone. It was clear in his tone and posture and now Rider did as well. "Well, have you?"

"Of course, my lord. Thank you."

Lord Quill opened his mouth to say something, but I wasn't going to wait for the dream to take a worse turn. I hurried down the path away from them and the courtyard packed with all those too-eager fae men. It was bad enough Lord Talon was the complete opposite of what he'd been in the Tower and now Rider — no *Lord* Rider since he was the Lord Commander of the Black Guard — was going back to the man I knew he really was.

CHAPTER 18
Quill

THE REDHEAD MURMURED her thank you, shocking me with how demure it was, and fled. She didn't seem unsteady on her feet, so she couldn't have been completely stunned by her soul manifesting in the garden, but she had looked like she was in shock. And Rider wouldn't have helped her if she'd been fine. He wasn't interested in doing anything with a woman — fae or human — and he'd never been interested in taking a mate.

The only woman he talked to was his sister, because if he got too friendly with anyone else, the Goddess, because he possessed powerful magic, would consider him a possible mate for any woman with awakened unbound mating marks, just like the redhead, whether he wanted a mate or not.

And she had all of her marks. None of her marks had shifted from her hair color to her eye color which meant she didn't have any mates yet.

Except that didn't matter for me. No matter how friendly I got, or even if she fell in love with me, the Goddess would never mate us. The odds of the Goddess even picking me as a last mate were almost non-existent since I didn't have any magic at all. It wasn't impossible, but a man without magic hadn't been mated for four hundred years and I doubted I'd be the one to change that.

Even if my current search did lead me to develop a magical ability, that didn't change the fact I might make a magicless child and there were already too many of us — and too many newborns — without the divine spark.

No, having a mate was beyond me. The best I could hope for was getting stronger and being an equal member of our command team. And right now, that meant figuring out why there were more shadows in the Gray and why they were more aggressive.

"That—" Rider growled, his gaze still locked on the path where the redhead had gone "—wasn't necessary."

"So, you *are* going to find her when we're done," Talon huffed. He wasn't interested in a mate either.

"Of course I'm not going after her. I've got more

important things to worry about." Rider jerked his attention away from the path and glared at Talon. "But she's so disoriented, I'm not even sure she knows where she is."

A strange mix of emotions flashed over Talon's expression. He wasn't an asshole. He did care about other people, but he couldn't do what Rider did and just avoid women. They flocked to him whether he wanted their attention or not and he had to be more aggressive to get them to look somewhere else. Which was why he'd been so sharp with the redhead.

"At least she can walk," Talon said. Which was as much of a peace offering as Rider was going to get.

Rider sighed and strode to the nearby benches where we were originally supposed to meet and sat. "I'm not sure that's a good thing. The *children* didn't notice her condition and swarmed her."

"Most women like that," Talon said, sinking onto the bench across from him.

"Do you?" Rider shot back, pointing out that Talon was often swarmed, especially in the human realm if he wasn't careful, and didn't enjoy it at all.

Talon shrugged, his gaze sliding to the path where the redhead had disappeared. "I'm not a woman."

"And this isn't what we're here to talk about," I said, jumping in before Rider could respond.

As much as I wanted to know more about the woman and was worried she wouldn't be all right, we needed to discuss the novices before they arrived. Which was the whole reason we were meeting in the Garden tonight and not waiting until tomorrow when I was in the Gray.

"Fine," Talon huffed, jerking his attention back to Rider. "How do you want to train the novices?"

"It can't be the same as usual," I said, sitting beside him. "We've lost too many men and we can't afford to keep them out of the full rotation for the regular two seasons."

"I know," Rider replied, his expression grim.

Talon only needed four replacements for his elite unit and I only needed two, but Rider had lost a dozen of his elite guard and close to another dozen of the regular guard since the last lottery. And almost all of them were human. We had more human novices this time than we'd ever had before— Hell, we had more novices than we'd ever had before, and we didn't have nearly enough time to train them properly.

"We should be able to put the fae novices straight into a modified rotation after initial assessments," I said, "But maybe there'll be a few humans who already have decent fighting abilities."

"Not if they're like the one who just arrived," Rider said. "Sure, he managed to kill a shadow hound, but he was stupid enough to use the ring after dark."

Talon's eyes widened. "You're talking about that

red-haired child who stumbled into the bathhouse covered in shadow blood? He killed a hound?"

Red hair? I'd delivered the summons to a redhead that afternoon. What were the odds Ash, the other guardsman who handed out summons, also had a redhead on his list of novices?

"Saw it with my own eyes and it was dumb luck," Rider huffed. "Dumb being the operative word."

"But that shows promise," Talon said, his expression darkening. "I know the humans think they're men at sixteen, but they're not. And he's small, even for a sixteen-year-old human male. If he managed to kill a hound, then we can work with that. He's young. He'll grow into a man soon enough."

"So, you're saying someone came through the ring after dark?" I asked, stunned.

We'd made it clear to the humans that it was suicide to come to the Gray after dark and their priests were supposed to pass that knowledge to every man in the lottery. The light created from the ring's magic was a beacon to all the shadows in the area. There was a slim chance someone could run to the Tower before he was swarmed, but that depended on how far away the shadows were, and with their increasing numbers, the odds that at least one of them was close to the ring was good. "Suicide attempt?"

"I don't think so," Talon replied. "He's... inexperienced, not stupid or suicidal."

"Yeah, and he better get *experienced* fast," Rider growled. "Next time we might not get so lucky and someone will get hurt. Unless of course, that idiot is Ash." Rider ran a hand over his face, already looking tired and the first rotation of training the novices hadn't even started. "I really hate when he plays the dumb ones."

CHAPTER 19
Quill

I HATED it when Ash played the dumb ones, too, but he usually wasn't dumb to the point of endangering someone. And stepping through the ring after dark endangered whoever had ridden out to save him. He had no way of knowing that Rider would be one of his rescuers, so couldn't have counted on Rider coming to his aid. Sure, because the novices arrived tomorrow Rider wouldn't be hunting with one of the elite teams tonight, but he also wouldn't have taken a position on the wall. I suspected it was just luck that Rider had been on the wall when the novice had arrived.

But Talon has said the novice had red hair and was young. I'd delivered a summons to a boy who fit that description that afternoon, which meant he couldn't be Ash, since Ash was out delivering summonses as well.

"I don't think this novice is Ash," I said.

Ash, with his magic to change his appearance, always disguised himself as a human novice for the first of the two seasons of novice training to help identify those who might be a problem once they were part of the regular rotation.

Because the humans didn't join the guard voluntarily like the fae, not everyone had the same skill level and some humans believed that meant their life was already over and attempted to end it, while others thought it gave them the right to make life more difficult for those weaker than themselves. Some fae believed that as well, but most were too afraid of Rider to create serious problems.

The problem was that Ash was damned good at what he did and, as much as we tried, we could never figure out who he was until he revealed himself as a potential target for those looking for someone to intimidate or an intimidator ready to join in. The only advantage we ever had was that Ash took two thirds of the list of summonses and hid himself among them, which meant there was always one third of the novices who I or Talon knew wasn't Ash because we'd delivered those summons ourselves.

"The boy's name is Sawyer Herstind, but I'm surprised he didn't wait until tomorrow to come to the Gray," I added, my mind jumping back to that moment.

It had been strange, unlike so many of the

summonses I'd made before. The woman with the same red hair as her brother had assured me there wouldn't be crying. It had almost felt as if she knew her brother's name would be called. But then she'd almost fainted, and every time I closed my eyes, I saw that look on her face when I'd grabbed her arm to steady her.

She'd looked up at me, and her eyes, brown but with a hint of impossible emerald flickering in their depths as if a part of me wanted her to actually be fae, were filled with shock and terror.

And then the Marquis had yelled at her and the terror had deepened for a moment before vanishing behind a mask of blank obedience.

"Sawyer Herstind?" Talon asked, his frown deepening. "As in Herstind March?"

"Yes. Probably a nephew to the Marquis." Which would explain why he'd been standing on that pretentious dais behind the Marquis... but didn't explain why he'd been treating Sawyer's sister like a servant. Even as his niece, the Marquis could solidify his political alliances by marrying her to someone important.

The thought left a bitter taste in my mouth. It was disgusting how humans treated their women, but we'd made an alliance with them. Even with half of our population possessing some form of magic, we still weren't strong enough to defend ourselves if the Shadow Gate opened again. We needed each other and neither of us were going to make demands for cultural changes and turned a blind eye, pretending we didn't notice.

"I didn't think the Marquis had any nephews fostering at Herstind castle," Talon said, his position in the Gold Tower giving him greater knowledge of the humans' political arrangements just like my position in the White Tower made me more knowledgeable on magical developments and research.

"And it doesn't matter," Rider said. "Whatever life he had before is over."

And his sister was now alone.

I didn't know where that thought had come from. I didn't know for certain that she was now alone, but given how the Marquis had treated her, I doubted anyone would stand against him for her sake.

Although given how young her brother was, I doubted he'd been any protection... except if what Rider said was true, the boy had killed a hound. That meant he had to have a spark in his soul. A spark that had probably been repressed by the Marquis.

"We need to test the novices and then split them up for their second rotation," Rider said. "As much as I'd like to hold back those who are more skilled to help bring up the abilities of the others, we can't afford to remain undermanned. All of the elite teams have lost a lieu day each rotation just to keep up with our losses. The men can't keep that up forever."

"We shouldn't wait for the novices to join the rotation," Talon said. "Start the competition for the elite positions and take from the guards who've already proven themselves."

"There's a Bond, a Mannerly, and a Wild in this year's list of novices," I said.

They were three of almost a dozen human families that didn't see going to the Gray as a punishment and trained their sons accordingly. There were other families that were scattered throughout the Five Great Human Kingdoms, but the Bond and Wild families were in Addur, the capital of Erellod, and were trained and treated like nobility even if they weren't — most likely because if a nobleman's son's name was drawn, someone from one of those families would take his place — while the Mannerly family was their equivalent in the capital of Irialas, one of the Five Great Kingdoms that bordered Erellod.

"A Bond, Mannerly, *and* a Wild?" Talon asked, surprising me since he usually looked at the list of names before the novices arrived even if it wasn't his year to hand out the summons.

Rider raised an eyebrow. "You haven't looked at the list?"

"I was going to look at it in the morning," Talon shot back. "Ash swamped me with reports about the human machinations going on in the Gold Tower during the kings' meeting, and I've been juggling that and security for Princess Edelina's betrothal party."

"That party is months away," Rider replied.

"And yet nobles are already arriving." Talon rolled his eyes.

A human betrothal was a chance to make political alliances, not just between the families getting married but between those who'd been invited. And while many nobles had their own security, it was the Guard's gold elites that were responsible for ensuring everyone's safety.

Which meant the sooner Talon's unit was back to their full compliment, the easier it would be to juggle security at the Gold Tower. That said—

"It would be a mistake to make highly trained novices wait for who-knows-how-many years to take an elite position," I said. "And two of them are from Addur. They'll likely have experience fighting together and be an asset on anyone's elite unit."

"Then we open it up to the novices as well," Talon suggested. "I need a full compliment for the princess's party. Extra men if you can spare them. And you need hunters."

Rider gave a tight nod. "Agreed. We'll divide the novices between skill level at the end of the first rotation, give them a chance to get their bearings. Then after a few rotations of getting them into shape we'll open up the training rotation for the competition to the regular grunts as well as the novices."

"And that training has to be two rotations not five before we start the competition," Talon added, which was great for him and Rider but terrible for me.

Sure, I only needed two men, but I needed men with more training than they did. Rider's hunters needed exceptional fighting abilities since they actively hunted the shadows, and Talon's men needed to know how to behave properly among human nobles. I needed men who could read and speak both human and fae at least at a basic level and understood the foundations of magic so they could properly protect — and not disrupt — the scholars researching and experimenting in the White Tower.

"I reserve the right to withhold judgement and demand extra training before selecting my men," I said. "I can't risk someone blowing up half of the White Tower because they couldn't read the label on a door." And I also couldn't have men who didn't respect a woman's authority. Unlike the humans, our women held positions of power greater than any man, and almost a quarter of the fae scholars at the White Tower were women. We even had a few female human scholars.

Which made me think of Sawyer's sister, alone in a place where I knew in my heart she was terrified and powerless.

She'd been demure, but there'd been a keenness in the way she looked at me, as if she could see more than just the Guardsman that I was. Perhaps if I took her to the White Tower, she'd have what it took to be a scholar's assistant or even a scholar. Then she wouldn't have to live in Herstind castle. She'd even be able to see her brother on his lieu days.

And why was I thinking about her? It couldn't be because I was desperate for a mate that I'd take a human. That would be ridiculous and wasn't fair to her. Women wanted children and a fae man couldn't give a human woman a child. We could barely give a fae woman a child. That and we lived hundreds of years longer than humans. We'd be childless and far-too-quickly I'd be alone again.

No, I was better off as I was with my brothers-in-arms: Rider, Ash, and Talon. And if I wanted sex, I could visit the brothel in the human realm that catered to the Guard, or be with Talon, who was always up for sex, be it with me or a human, or with me *and* a human.

Except that only made me think of me with Talon and Sawyer's sister, turning that look of fear in her eyes to one of pure pleasure.

CHAPTER 20

Sage

THE PATH I'd run down to get away from Rider, Talon, and Lord Quill ended up skirting around the edge of a wing of the tree-building to a magical grove with bathing pools. The ground turned into a rocky, multi-tiered slope with multiple pools on each tier and paths that wound around thick bushes and wide tree trunks, implying more pools lay beyond. The largest pool, halfway down, had two women and a dozen men fawning over them, while smaller groups of men bathed in a few of the other pools.

Steam curled from most of the pools, but not all and to varying degrees, indicating different tempera-tures, and for a moment I couldn't figure out how that was possible before remembering this was a dream. I'd turned the bathhouse underneath the Black Tower into a magical grove filled with fae almost as gorgeous as Lord Talon and who were all staring at me. Including the women.

One of them looked at me with joy, her expression inviting, while the other stared daggers at me. The one staring daggers cleared her throat and the dozen men in the pool with her all jerked their attention back to her, making the three men, clustered tightly together in a nearby smaller pool, chuckle. They, however, also went back to what they were doing which looked like—

The prelude to sex with two of them kissing while the third—

I heaved my attention away. I didn't know if my imagination would fill in the rest or if the dream would take a weird turn, and I wasn't prepared for either.

One of the men in another pool that was out in the open stood. The water lapped around his thighs, drawing my attention to his cock — which for some reason wasn't as impressive as the only cock I'd ever gotten a good look at — and he held out his hand to me in invitation.

"You're new," he purred, just like Black Hair had when I'd first arrived. He also had the same hunger in his eyes that made my insides squirm with unease. "Join us."

The other man with him stood as well, as if giving me an eyeful of their stunning, sculpted bodies was what I needed to make my decision.

"Ah... no. Not tonight," I stammered and hurried along the path, away from the grove... which was the stupidest thing I could have done. I had two naked men, ready and willing to entertain me.

Except even if they were my imagination, they didn't *feel* right.

There was something dangerous about them, something that made me fear my dream would take a horrible turn.

That, and I couldn't bring myself to have sex out in the open with everyone watching, dream or no dream. And without a doubt the dream would turn sour and Talon would walk around the corner and catch me and that would be even more embarrassing than having been caught staring at his cock in real life.

I reached an arch that was an impossible mix of stone and living tree and stepped into another strange grove. This was a maze of passages with doors and curtains, partial rooms, dimly lit alcoves, and nooks with cushioned lounges.

The steady warm glow of the fae lights that had gently illuminated the garden dimmed a bit in here and turned into a soft pink, lighting the way with the soft light from the glowing white and pink flowers growing along a vine that entwined around everything: over arches, around silver fences and screens.

The warm breeze sighed, rustling the thick canopy of leaves above me and tickling through the flowers, making their gentle light dance on the stone path and walls, and a sense of peace and warmth filled me as light flickered from the spots on my skin.

There was something sacred about where I was. I didn't know how to explain it, but I could feel.... magic? Was that what it was?

Whatever it was, it caressed my skin and seeped into me. It sank into the core of my being, adding fuel to a spark in my chest that I hadn't realized was there then turned into a heat that radiated from my heart through my limbs to my fingers and toes.

I wandered deeper into the grove, savoring the strange warm sensation sliding within me, watching the light from the flowers dance every time the breeze brushed them, and catching glimpses of light flickering from the spots trailing from my neck down the inside curve of my breasts.

This was how a dream was supposed to be. Warm and soft and comfortable with none of my real-life worries about being discovered or not being desirable or not having an ally in the Black Tower.

The path led past a series of three, intricately carved wooden doors, two on the left, one on the right, then turned a corner and split into two paths.

I was about to pick the path to the right, when I realized there weren't two paths but three, one on the far left that was narrower than the other two and partially hidden by the flowering vines.

I slipped between the vines onto the narrower path, the walls so close together I could easily reach out and trail my fingers through the blooms on both sides of me.

There were fewer flowers here and no fae lights, and the shadows deepened, but I didn't get a sense that the dream was going to shift from warm and peaceful to something dangerous.

The path branched off a few times into paths just as narrow and dimly lit as the one I followed and finally ended in a diamond shaped nook.

The flowering vine filled the nook, trailing over all walls and even on the ground, but the light from the flowers was muted, barely glowing, and the canopy of leaves above had pulled away, framing the edges of the nook and offering an unobstructed view of a stunning night sky speckled with stars. In the center sat a cushioned backless bench with wide, gently sloped arms so someone — or two someones if they cuddled together — could lean back and stare at the stars in comfort.

I stepped off the smoothed-stone path onto soft, dark moss, and headed toward the bench. But movement out of the corner of my eye and soft sighing caught my attention, drawing me toward a flicker of light coming through the vines.

The vines that were thick everywhere else in the nook thinned in this one spot, entwining around a silver fence and framing the room on the other side.

Inside, the light from the flowers was brighter than the light in the nook, enough for me to see clearly, but still soft enough to suggest seductive intimacy. Two men — one completely naked, one just in his pants — stood in the center of the room with a naked fae woman, caressing and kissing her.

Light flickered from the silver spots trailing around her neck, over her collarbone, and down between her breasts. With her long black hair hanging loose down her back in a veil offering teasing glimpses of her body every time the men brushed it, I knew I was watching Rider's sister — or the woman who I'd turned into Rider's sister because this was a dream and I had no idea if Rider even had a sister.

Beyond, on an enormous bed with white sheets and a variety of green pillows of various shades and sizes was another man, also completely naked. He lounged on his side in the center and watched Lark and the other two men. He slowly stroked his hand up and down an impressive erection, his dark eyes filled with a searing, heated desire, while another man sat on a cushioned couch in the corner, fully dressed, with a similar look in his eyes—

No, stronger, darker, more intense. It was as if Lark was the only woman for him and he needed her more than he needed to breathe. The look made my chest ache with a yearning I hadn't realized I had.

I wanted someone to look at me like that, to love

me so completely that I knew without a doubt I could trust him with everything: my life, my hopes, my truth. I wanted someone to accept me for who I was, who embraced the fact that I didn't want to do the things expected of a woman, who saw me as an equal, who listened and respected my thoughts and desires.

Which was why this was all a dream, a fantasy to remind me that even though I'd escaped from Edred, my life still wasn't my own and there was no one I could trust.

CHAPTER 21

Sage

I LEANED my cheek against the vine-wrapped fence and watched, my heart aching, imagining it was me captured between those two gorgeous men, their sculpted muscles pressed against me, their hands roaming, caressing, making me sigh against their lips.

The completely naked man with Lark shifted behind her, his lips trailing across her jaw. He drew her long hair away from her neck and pressed gentle kisses on the glowing spots there, making her eyelids flutter shut and sending a shiver of need rushing through me.

His dark brown hair was cut short, like Lord Quill's, but he had a similar build to Talon and the same stunning sculpted physique. Silver spots encircled both of his biceps, the color bright against his medium brown skin, and pulsed in time with the spots on Lark's neck. In fact, all the men — except for the man still fully dressed whose biceps I couldn't see — had silver spots encircling their upper arms.

The other man tangled his fingers in Lark's hair and captured her lips in a deep, breathtaking kiss. She moaned into his mouth and rocked her hips forward, pressing her mound against what I fantasized was a rock-hard erection. It was difficult to tell with her body partially blocking him and his pants still on, but the two naked men were fully aroused, and if I was going to fantasize, the other two would be hard and ready as well.

My need deepened and blossomed into a soft, slick ache between my thighs. What would it feel like to have their hard length pushing inside me. Would they go slow, drawing out the sensation? Or would they be quick and hurried like Royston had been?

No. This was a fantasy. They'd go slowly, their eyes filled with a desire just for me, their bodies a tool to worship me, to show me I was precious and desirable.

They would tease me first, just like the men were teasing Lark, but in the end, I'd be filled with a glorious bliss, just like how it was described in the minstrels' tales and our hearts would be entwined by true love.

I bit back a moan of desire, my body throbbing with a need that wasn't going to be fulfilled anytime soon.

Jeez. Talon had definitely awakened something

within me that I hadn't known was there. I'd never had an erotic dream like this before. Yes, a few fantasies about finding someone, about sex being as delicious and romantic as the tales claimed and not the fast disappointment it had been with Royston.

But the dreams had never been this clear before, never with multiple men at the same time, and never with the hope of finding that one true love that had never been and was never going to be my fate.

The men drew Lark to the bed. She settled on the soft mattress and the third man took over kissing her lips as the other two men started teasing her nipples with mouths and tongues and fingers. The man on the couch huffed, a low throaty sound that sounded almost animalistic, and loosened the ties on the front of his pants so he could shove his hand inside, his gaze never leaving Lark.

The ache between my legs grew, along with an ache in my breasts. I imagined the heat and rasp of their tongues and the delicious pinch as they sucked on my— *her* nipples. Her head tipped back in pleasure and the man possessing her lips deepened their kiss, breathing in her gasps and moans.

Then both of the men worshiping her nipples slid a hand down her body and started teasing the inside of her thighs, their fingers drawing closer and closer to her core.

My breath picked up in anticipation. The boy I'd

been with before hadn't played between my legs with his fingers, but I'd caught one of Edred's men in an alcove with his fingers buried inside one of the castle's maids which was how I had to be dreaming about this. The maid hadn't looked like she enjoyed the attention as much as Lark was, but I imagined with the right man and the right intention, Lark's experience was what it should be like.

And now I ached for a man to touch me there as well— hell, just to touch me with desire.

Which was the truth of this dream that a part of me didn't want to admit.

I'd never been touched or looked at with the desire that the men with Lark had for her, and now I was surrounded by men who, even when they did discover I was a woman, wouldn't look at me like that.

Because they'd know the truth. I wasn't beautiful or feminine. I wouldn't make a good wife and I didn't want to be one. I wanted to be in control of my own destiny, not told what to do and who to have sex with by Edred or any man. I didn't want to look at my feet or smile meekly or be obedient.

But I still wanted to be desired. I wanted to be strong *and* loved. I wanted—

Things I was never going to have.

And the sooner I accepted that, the sooner I could focus on what was important, which was keeping my secret long enough for Sawyer to escape.

Then...

Well then, I guess if I was lucky, I'd be sent back to Edred and punished. And with my luck, he'd figure out how to keep my *indiscretion* a secret so he could still sell my hand in marriage for an advantageous alliance.

I closed my eyes on my desires laid bare in front of me and tried to force myself to turn away. Watching Lark and those men wasn't a fantasy. It was a way to torture myself, showing me what I yearned for and could never have.

But someone stepped up close behind me, startling me before I could leave, and I froze, my eyes snapping open and locking again on the three men pleasuring Lark.

"Like what you see?" a masculine voice, edged with a playful hint of amusement, murmured in my ear.

His breath feathered across my cheek and neck, sending a shiver of need rushing straight to my core, as my pulse lurched into a rapid tattoo. I'd been caught. Was the dream going to punish me for peeping?

"I ah..." Heat blazed across my cheeks and I tried to jerk away, but he clasped his hands over mine, securing me to the fence and boxing me in with his arms, making me hyperaware of how big he was — just like all the fae men I'd encountered so far.

Unable to escape, I dropped my gaze, instinct kicking in and making me behave demurely. "I didn't mean to pry."

"You're not," he murmured, hooking a finger under my chin and urging me to look up again.

I didn't fight him, but I didn't open my eyes, either.

"If Lark wanted privacy, she'd have picked one of the fully walled-in rooms. But she doesn't care if someone watches and two of her mates get excited at the thought. This room, where someone can peek but isn't out in the open, is her compromise with the two of her mates who are more modest." He chuckled. "It's all right to watch. It's all right to be excited by watching."

Lark released a long, sensual moan, and my eyelids flickered open of their own volition. One of the men still sucking on her breasts had slid two fingers inside her, while the other one rubbed her sensitive nub.

"Blaze really likes to watch." He nudged my chin, turning my attention to the man on the couch. He'd fully freed his large, thick erection, and was gripping it tightly. "He'll try and hold out for as long as possible, working himself up but refusing to come until he's buried inside her. Which with this being the first time in a season that he's been able to be in the Garden in physical form with her, isn't going to be long."

The thought sent another shudder rushing through me. He — Blaze — practically vibrated with need, his body tight, his eyes filled with a hunger that promised an overwhelming assault of sensation when he finally broke and made love to her.

"Hmmm, you like that," the man behind me

purred... and for some reason his purr didn't scare me like it had with all the other fae men. It turned me on.

But then I was watching sensual, erotic lovemaking, and we were in a private, intimate alcove. Perhaps this was what I needed to embrace my dream and fulfill desires I knew would never be fulfilled in real life.

"I like what that promises," I replied.

"Hard and fast?"

"Powerful. Consuming." Worshiped. Loved.

"You like to be dominated?" he asked, his breath caressing my cheek and neck again.

The thought of being dominated by Blaze made my core ache... but the thought of being dominated by someone like Edred twisted cold in my gut.

"Ah, it depends on the man," he murmured, as if he'd heard my thoughts. And with this being a dream, he probably had. "Blaze's kind of desire does require Lark to completely trust him. What about the others?"

My attention jumped from Blaze back to the bed where the man with the short brown hair was sensually sliding his fingers in and out of her. Her breath had picked up, her moans coming faster as her pleasure grew making my own desire swell.

The man who'd been kissing her before had traded places with the one who'd been sucking her nipples and she had her hands clenched in his hair as her body rocked with her rising need. Then she tensed and cried her release.

My need tightened in response, my body aching for that same kind of pleasure. A soft moan escaped my lips, and I leaned back against the man who'd captured me against the vine-covered fence, my body searching for its own release.

"Do you want me to touch you?" he asked, his voice soft with no hint of a predatory purr, giving me the sense that even though I was pressed against him, if I said no he wouldn't do anything, and he wouldn't press the matter and try to convince me.

But I *did* want him to touch me. I wanted him to make me feel how it looked like Lark was feeling. I wanted to satisfy the craving Talon had awoken that had filled my dream from the moment I'd opened my eyes in this beautiful, strange garden. I was never going to get anything so incredible in real life because sex wasn't like that, and I wasn't a woman that men desired, so I might as well get it in my dreams.

CHAPTER 22

Sage

"Yes," I replied, my voice breathy and filled with yearning. "Touch me. Make me feel like that."

"And how does that feel?" he murmured, teasing his fingers into my long hair and brushing it away from the side of my neck. His warm breath fluttered against my skin, and I ached for him to complete the move and press his lips against my pulse.

"Good." *And cherished and seen.*

He brushed his lips against my neck and warmth flickered in my spots, sending sensual heat swelling in my core and making my breath hitch.

"Just good?" he chuckled, the sound warm and sensual, adding to the heat growing within me. "I can do better than that."

He tangled his fingers in my hair and captured my lips in a sudden kiss. It was shocking and consuming from the beginning, nothing soft and tentative about it, reminding me of the searing desire in Blaze's eyes.

His lips were hard and commanding, and his tongue invaded my mouth, forcefully deepening our connection.

The sudden assault was overwhelming and stole my breath. I'd never been kissed like that before. Royston had been uncertain and awkward. There hadn't actually been a lot of kissing. There hadn't been much of anything, really.

Then the man slipped his hand inside the front of my dress, roughly palming my breast, and the shock swept into hot, aching need. Fantasy Man wasn't going to be anything like Royston, he was going to be... well, my fantasy.

Except when I moved to cup his cheek and reciprocate his touch, he captured my wrist and pressed my hand back against the fence.

"Oh no," he said, his voice low and husky. "Do you see Lark doing any of the work?"

My gaze jumped to Lark and the three men on the bed. She still lay on the center of the mattress with her black hair splayed out like a dark halo on the white sheets, and her silver spots radiating a strange shimmering white light that was matched on the men's arms. The men had rearranged themselves. Now the man who'd had his fingers inside her made love to her mouth while the guy still in his pants lay between her legs, trailing kisses up the inside of her thigh, and the third fondled her breasts. She had one hand tangled in the hair of the man at her breasts and her other hand wrapped around the cock of the man kissing her.

"Yes." I pushed my free hand between me and Fantasy Man and rubbed my palm against the hard — and oh Great Father, huge! — bulge in the front of his pants.

He groaned, captured that hand and put it back on the fence with the other one, boxing me in again. "This is supposed to make *you* feel good."

"I think you're allow to take pleasure in this as well," I breathed as the man kissing Lark's thigh inched closer and closer to her entrance.

Blaze growled low in his throat, drawing my attention. His breath was fast and his hand on his cock was tight and trembling, while his other hand dug into the cushions beside him. His desire for her was ferocious, darkening his eyes with an almost animalistic hunger.

"Unless you're like Blaze," I said, realization suddenly hitting me, "and like to torture yourself first."

"Not really my style," Fantasy Man purred. "And Blaze usually has better control than this, even if it has been a while for him. The priestess must have blessed the pool tonight. That usually makes him more... hungry."

"So let me touch you," I said.

"Nope. This is for you. Consider it a welcome to the

Garden gift," he replied, his lips brushing against my neck as his hands dipped back into my dress.

I moaned softly, and more blissful heat swelled within me at his touch. He hummed a low, sensual sound of pure masculine satisfaction, and rocked his hips against my rear, pressing his hard length against me. Would he be just as impressive as Talon or the men with Lark? He felt just as impressive. And of course he'd know exactly what to do with it.

His fingers plucked at my nipples with a delicious spike of pain that seemed to snap from my breasts straight to my core.

I released a louder moan, my eyelids fluttering shut with pleasure, and he pressed his body harder against mine as if he was starting to get swept up in the moment and forget that he was supposed to be focused entirely on my pleasure.

On the other side of the fence someone gasped and Blaze growled. My eyes snapped open — I hadn't even realized I'd let them close — and my breath caught.

The man who'd been teasing the inside of Lark's thighs had stretched out on the bed and buried his face between her legs. His tongue flicked out, swiping against her and she gasped again as her eyes rolled back in pleasure.

"Women can have that too?" I breathed.

Just like I'd caught one of Edred's men feeling up a maid, I'd also seen a few maids on their knees with

LIES WITHIN THE DARKEST TOWER   171

men's cocks in their mouths. The men had looked like they'd enjoyed it and a couple of the maids had as well, but I hadn't thought a man would offer the same kind of pleasure to a woman.

Because that was all it was. Pleasure for a woman. The man might be more aroused — and from the look in Blaze's eyes and the eyes of the other men they were certainly aroused watching — but they wouldn't get a release. And it looked like Lark was well on her way to another one.

It was the most erotic, sensual thing I'd ever seen and it made my pulse pound. My body throbbed and my mouth went dry in anticipation. I ached to know what that would feel like, prayed it would be as amazing as it looked, and feared that because this was a dream it would turn into a disappointment.

"Who's been teaching you about sex?" Fantasy Man asked. "That's one of the best parts." Which of course he'd say because he was my fantasy dream man.

He stilled, his hands firm around my breasts, his lips teasing my neck, and his erection hard against me. "Have you never had sex before?"

A chill rushed through me. Would he stop if I said I hadn't? Was this how the dream was going to turn into a nightmare. Except—

"I've had sex," I said as the man between Lark's legs nuzzled closer and did something that made her hips rock into him and her back arch off the bed. "I've just never had it like that before."

"Well then." Fantasy Man released me and stepped back, sending regret and frustration rushing through me.

"Hey—" I started to turn to demand he return, but he dropped to his knees instead of walking away — or disappearing like most of the men in my dreams — and reached for the hem of my dress.

"We need to fix this right away," he said without looking up at me.

He pulled the skirt of my dress over his head, pressed his hands against my ankles, and slid them slowly up the inside of my legs, urging me to make room for him.

My pulse skipped a beat. He was really going to kiss me *there*. But of course, he was. This was a dream. And if I could just hold on to this, it would be the most incredible dream I'd ever had.

He turned and settled between my legs, his back against the fence, and trailed his fingers closer and closer to my core.

My breathing hitched and my legs trembled.

Oh yes. Oh yes oh yes oh yes.

I clung to the fence as his hot breath followed his fingers up my right thigh, drawing closer and closer. Lark moaned and writhed and the man between her legs grabbed her hips, mercilessly licking and sucking, turning her breath ragged.

Then Fantasy Man's tongue, hot and wet, with just a hint of friction, teased against my sensitive nub, sudden and shocking. It sent sensation zinging through me. I gasped and the gaze of the guy whose cock was captured in Lark's grasp, flickered toward me then back to Lark. The look in his eyes darkened even more and a shudder swept through him.

"Don't," Blaze snarled, making the guy suck in sharp breaths, trying to control his release. "The pool was blessed. Your seed could be the one we need."

The man nodded, sucking in more sharp breaths, but Fantasy Man teased his tongue against me again, sending more sensation rushing through me and making my eyes rolled back with pleasure before I could see if the man managed to regain control of himself.

And really, as much as watching those three men pleasure Lark made me throb with need, I didn't need to watch anymore. I had my own man, and the feel of his strong hands on the inside of my thighs and his hot breath on my flesh was incredible.

I let my head loll back and clung to the fence, the rough vine digging into my palms. Fantasy Man brushed his fingers along the seam of my leg, drawing achingly close to my slit and tortured me with his tongue, quick, sudden flicks that shocked with a promise of the sensation that was about to come and drew more gasps that I tried to control so as not to draw the notice of the men with Lark.

I'd already made the mistake of being too loud and one of them already knew I was watching them and was turned on. I didn't want all of them to know and I didn't want the dream to change to something else.

But then Fantasy Man gave a long, slow, powerful lick, and my heated need surged, stealing my breath.

He licked and sucked, making me fight to hold in my gasps and moans, until I was trembling, twisted so tight I was sure I'd come.

My breathing had turned ragged, and he hummed with that delicious sound of masculine satisfaction that only turned me on more. It shocked me that even in my dream, my fantasy man would find pleasure in just bringing me pleasure, but he never asked for more and he clearly wasn't rushing.

He brought me to the edge of what I was sure was going to be a release as incredible as the one Lark had already had, then eased back, teasing me with little breaths and flicks before building me up again.

He kept me teetering on the edge until I feared I was never going to get a release and the dream was going to keep me on the precipice, never satisfied. It was even crueler than my experience with Royston. He'd never brought me pleasure like this, never made me feel like I was on the edge of something incredible. He'd just teased me a little then took his own pleasure. This was... incredible and cruel and breathtaking—

And then Fantasy Man slid a finger inside me and stared licking and sucking with a frenzy that made me think of Blaze. If I managed to open my eyes, pull my skirt back, and look down would I see the same hunger in Fantasy Man's eyes that I'd seen in Blaze's?

Great Father I wanted that, and yet I didn't want to be disappointed if it wasn't there... and I wasn't sure I'd be able to let go of the fence and keep standing to look.

Fantasy Man hummed and sighed and twisted my need tighter and tighter. I couldn't catch my breath, my whole body trembled, and I no longer cared if anyone saw or heard me. The only thing I could think about was the promise of something amazing building within me, its whirling, growing sensation.

A final, sudden explosion tossed me from the edge Fantasy Man had brought me to again and again, and I gasped, surprised. Hot, liquid bliss roared through me, and I released a long loud moan. Lights flashed behind my lids and my essence spun around and around and around.

I'd never felt so boneless, so incredible, so sexy. I was sensation and light and power, and I didn't want to think about the fact that this was just a dream, and my reality was cold and hard and disappointing. I wanted to stay in this moment forever but knew that was impossible. I could only hope that I'd be able to have this dream again.

CHAPTER 23

Ash

THE WOMAN TENSED and sucked in a surprised gasp as if she hadn't known what it was like to come. Then she released a long, loud moan that I had no doubt Lark and every one of her mates heard even in the throes of their lovemaking.

I pushed back the skirt of the redhead's gauzy red dress so I could look at her. She clung to the fence as if that was the only thing holding her up and her head had dropped forward. Her breathing was ragged, her small breasts heaving against the front of her dress, reminding me how much I wanted to free them from that barely-there fabric and suck on them, while light blazed from her mating marks, illuminating the look of pure bliss on her delicate features. It stole my breath and brought me even closer to coming myself.

Goddess above. All I wanted now was to bend her

over the arm of the cushioned, backless bench in the middle of the nook and bury myself inside her.

But her spirit form shuddered and melted away, taking everything, her body and her cum around my mouth, and left me with only the memory of her luscious taste and her sweet moans.

I tipped my head back on the fence and closed my eyes. My own breathing was too fast, my cock hard and aching.

That had been a terrible mistake.

I shouldn't have teased her and I certainly shouldn't have offered to touch her. But she'd been watching Lark and her mates with such awe and need as if she'd never seen or experienced sex before. And it had been so long since I'd been with my own kind.

I ran my hands over my face and was suddenly too aware of the fact that my left side was smooth and normal, and my right side wasn't.

The rough, red scar that covered the right half of my face, ran down my neck, over my shoulder, covered my right pec, and showed up even in my spirit form, as if the results of that horrible night had been burned into my soul as well as my body. And with the Garden affecting my magic, making it difficult to change how I looked, I couldn't hide the truth from any woman. Not that I'd want to hide who I really was from my mate, but I couldn't even hide it long enough for a little sex.

My only hope was to find a woman who was new to

the Garden who didn't know me and had never gotten a chance to get a good look at me.

Which had been something I'd been avoiding up until now.

It hadn't felt right, like I was taking advantage of someone who didn't deserve it, and I'd avoided going through with it... up until now.

I had no idea why I'd been unable to resist this redhead. From the look of her, she was very new, and was perfect for the plan I hadn't really wanted to try. I didn't recognize her, and her spirit form kept flickering as if she didn't have enough experience holding it together. This was probably her first time in the Garden, and I'd been selfish, satisfying a desire I'd been able to ignore for years.

Except I hadn't satisfied the desire at all.

After not being with a fae woman for half a century and getting a taste of her, I wanted more. From talking with the others, I knew they didn't connect with fae woman the way I did, which only made my situation more cruel. I felt a power, a sense of peace, a promise of something incredible when I was with a fae woman. Something I didn't feel with a fae man or a human woman.

But with almost three quarters of the fae population being male, females had their pick of lovers, and why would any of them take a lover who couldn't even look normal in his spirit form when they could have someone like Talon?

Even Quill with no magic who the Goddess would never bond to a woman at least got invitations from unmated women for a little fun or women with mates looking for another to join them for a night of sex. And if I was too scary to look at, then no one would fall in love with me, and the Goddess would never consider me a potential mate for anyone.

Lark cried out Blaze's name in pleasure, making my cock scream for a release. Blaze snarled, his feline nature overwhelming him and the sounds of flesh slapping against flesh grew louder and faster.

He hadn't lasted long at all. But then he'd said the pool had been blessed and Lark and her mates had been trying to conceive for almost sixty years now. I knew it was a scar on Blaze's soul that he and the others hadn't be able to give her the one thing she'd always wanted.

Most fae women conceived at least once within their first thirty years of being mated, and every year that passed, the odds that Lark would conceive got smaller and smaller.

And while I wasn't sure I wanted a family, I did want a mate. My soul cried for that connection, the one I always felt at the edge of my senses when I made love with a fae woman.

But that life had been taken from me, and if I was

smart, I wouldn't torture myself by watching Lark with her mates or lose my control and play with anymore new arrivals.

Footsteps on the path outside of the nook drew my attention to the opening. They were soft, barely audible, but I'd trained myself to notice and pay attention to the slightest sounds — I was the spymaster and assassin of the Black Guard, and it would look terrible if I was ever caught unaware.

"Torturing yourself by watching Lark have sex?" Talon whispered as he stepped into the nook.

No, I'm torturing myself by making the new arrival come on my face.

I offered him a lazy shrug, trying to look as if nothing bothered me, but his eyes narrowed, seeing right through me.

"Maybe humans just aren't enough," I said, "Maybe I need a little more, even if I'm just watching."

Except I needed even more than that. I didn't get a connection from just watching, only a heightened sense of the memory of what the connection felt like, which was why I broke down and watched — sometimes even jerking off while watching.

The image of the redhead's face filled with bliss, her body trembling, her cum sweet on my tongue, swept through me, and my cock strained against the front of my pants. Goddess, I was a fool to have thought I could taste her and not want more.

CHAPTER 24

Ash

TALON'S GAZE flickered to my crotch, my erection obvious even in the dim light. "We both know your drought with fae woman is your own choice."

I swept a hand over the scars on my face. "Pretty sure no woman is attracted to this."

"When was the last time you actually tried?" Talon cocked a sculpted white eyebrow knowing full well that I hadn't tried to court anyone since I'd been burned.

The look of horror on the faces of the first two women who'd seen me enter the Garden after I'd recovered had been more than enough. I hadn't been able to hide the truth with my magic and the damned scars had shown up in my spirit form. My days of courting and hoping that the Goddess would bind me to a mate, like most fae men, were over.

"Well, be careful. Rider will beat you up if he catches you watching his sister," Talon said, sitting on the bench, leaning back on the arm — the same arm I wanted to bend the redhead over — and stared up at the stars. "Even if we all know his sister gets off on being watched."

Lark moaned again and out of the corner of my eye I saw her on her hands and knees with Flint slowly pushing into her. If I hadn't watched this bonded quintet have sex before, it would have surprised me that the soft-spoken, shy healer would like this particular position... although maybe it wasn't Flint who really liked it. Lark's mating marks always glowed brighter when one of her guys took her from behind.

"And he'll use his claws," Talon added.

I huffed. Rider probably would. He was almost as over-protective of Lark as her mates were, but then sisters were rare in the fae world.

"Then let's hope he doesn't like getting off by watching his sister have sex and come by for a peek," I drawled, certain he wouldn't.

I wasn't even sure if Rider was interested in sex at all, which was highly unusual for a fae, let alone a fae with an animal form. Most fae who could shift into an animal were aggressive and possessive and sexually hungry like Blaze.

And while Rider was aggressive, as growly as the wolf he turned into, I'd never seen him with a woman or heard of him with one. He didn't even join his men in Lehyrst in the human realm to visit the brothel and it had been over a hundred years since he'd been with Talon. And I still had no idea what had happened between them to end their relationship.

Flint groaned his satisfaction, the sound shooting straight to my cock. I needed to release the pressure, but to do that, Talon needed to get the hell out of here. And while I was sure if I asked, he'd be up for a fuck — he always was with anyone — what I wanted was to push into something hot and tight, like the redhead, and Talon preferred to be on top.

"Let's just get this conversation over with," I said, my tone sharper than I wanted.

Talon rolled his eyes at me. "You really are torturing yourself. When the novices get lieu time, you better be in the group that goes to Lehyrst and get that taken care of."

"If that's what my novice would do," I said, shifting in an attempt to ease the pressure of my throbbing cock.

"No one's met him yet, so decide now that he'd be just as lustful as most human males who think they're never going to get laid again."

Which was sad but true. The human novices when they first arrived always thought because they'd been selected for the Guard that they were never going to have sex with a woman again. They thought they were walking into a death sentence and were always shocked to find out life in the Guard was usually better than the life they'd been forced to leave behind.

With the exception of having to leave their family and not being able to marry and have children, along with the dangers of the job, they were healthier and better cared for than if they'd stayed in their village or town.

The only ones who had serious trouble adjusting were the sons of noblemen and they were the main reason I took a human form every year and underwent novice training for at least a season. Although that wasn't to say there weren't commoners who also caused problems, but if there was going to be someone still stuck in the humans' social hierarchy, it'd be the nobles.

Which was something I should be focusing on. But Talon wanted to talk about the latest reports I'd sent him, and I'd agreed to meet him in this nook after he'd met with Rider and Quill.

Lark's moans and sighs and the grunts from her mates grew louder.

I'd picked this nook because that conception room was usually empty and very few people knew about this place. There were other rooms that Lark and Blaze preferred more, so I hadn't expected them here, and I certainly hadn't expected to find that stunning redhead watching them.

I shoved that thought aside before I remembered the redhead's sighs and moans and taste again.

"You wanted to talk," I forced out, managing to keep my voice even this time.

I was supposed to be good at keeping my cool. But making the redhead come had shaken something within me and I couldn't seem to pull myself back together.

"I need you to get more information on the Jerika family," Talon replied. "The princess's betrothal party isn't for another few months and the oldest Jerika sister has already sent another retainer and a priest to join the first one to try to arrange a meeting with the King of Erellod."

"And you're afraid someone will try another assassination attempt on her son?" I asked.

The Jerika family was in the middle of a heated dispute that had been going on for years since the widowed Marquis, his childless heir, along with his heir's wife had died of the sweating sickness. The march should have gone to his brother — bypassing four older sisters — but the man had gone on a sailing expedition and hadn't returned. Now the Jerika family was fighting among themselves with various members struggling to take control of the land while others were still holding out hope for the rightful heir to return.

Last summer, someone had poisoned the oldest sister's oldest son at his betrothal party, nearly killing him and succeeding in killing his betrothed. He was the most likely candidate to become the Marquis of Jerika, old enough to actually hold the title without a male relative governing until he was of age.

But the second oldest sister had been given a better marital match, and her husband — who had an heir from a previous marriage — held a higher noble rank in the kingdom. She believed even though her son was still underage, he should become the next marquis because his father was a duke. And while I didn't have concrete proof, it looked like she was willing to do anything — include killing her nephew — to ensure her son took the title.

"I'm afraid of an assassination attempt and retaliation."

Which was highly likely. Jerika March was small but wealthy and whoever controlled it had a significant say in Erellod's economic and political decisions.

"I've been trying to get a man into the older sister's entourage but haven't had any luck." She'd become far more suspicious since the assassination attempt and had closed ranks, not letting someone she hadn't known for years and who hadn't been thoroughly vetted near her son. "We still have a few months, but we might just have to do with the men I have in the Gold Tower."

Talon's eyes narrowed. "If this family brings their feud to the Gold Tower, I don't know if I'm going to have enough men to deal with it."

And he couldn't necessarily count on any of the men in the Kings' Guard who supplemented his guard. They were all second and third sons from noble families in the Five Great Human Kingdoms and any one of them could have a connection to the Jerika family.

Except I only had so many men as well, and Rider had already gone to the kings of the Five Great Kingdoms and petitioned for an increase in the size of the Black Guard last summer and been denied. The human kings didn't want to sacrifice anymore men, and the High Priestess wasn't willing to commit more fae to the Guard if the humans weren't. Then, to top off the bad feelings with the Kingdoms, we'd asked for more names to be drawn in the lottery than ever before.

"The White Tower has been quiet." Too quiet, but perhaps I was just being paranoid. "I'll reassign one of my men in the White Tower to help with the Gold Tower."

Talon sighed. It was the best I could do and he knew it. If we weren't about to be training novices, I'd also be able to help gather information about the political machinations happening at the Gold Tower, but I'd skipped infiltrating the novices fifteen years ago and had one human commit suicide before his first season of training was done while two more had beaten another one to death.

Rider had sworn that would never happen again and given me the assignment to assassinate anyone who posed a threat to the rest of the men. Here was hoping I wouldn't have to kill anyone this year.

CHAPTER 25
Sage

FOOTSTEPS outside my door jerked me awake, sending pain throbbing through my chest and head, and for a moment I couldn't remember where I was. Darkness filled the strange narrow room, the only light coming from under the door and a small, strange glimmer on the wall. Then a loud, deep resonant *bong* from a large bell sounded and my thoughts lurched.

That was the first bell.

I was in the Black Tower.

The people outside my door were men who couldn't learn who I really was, and I was naked... and boneless and aching between my thighs from the most sensual dream I'd ever had.

Heat burned my face. One eyeful of Talon and I was fantasizing about sex in a way I'd never fantasized about before. Even my legs ached as if I'd actually been trembling and fighting to stay standing while that fae fantasy man had brought me to the most incredible climax.

A distinctly feminine sigh escaped my lips and the sensual ache within me froze. I couldn't ever make a sound like that again. But Great Father I wanted to. I wanted to go back to that dream, revel in the sensations, and be worshiped by that man's mouth again and again.

Shadows, what was wrong with me? I'd never wanted those things before.

Except I'd never seen a fae before, and Talon had said his magic awakened desires in humans.

So, all I had to do was avoid Talon. Which had to be why he'd been mean to me in my dream... before the dream had turned erotic and amazing and—

And I wasn't going to think about it ever again. Ever.

I unclenched my hands — hands still closed tight like they'd been when I'd been clinging to the fence — and a softly shimmering pink petal slid from my palm.

My pulse stuttered.

I hadn't noticed any flowers anywhere in the Tower, and while I'd been tired after I'd finally scrubbed my clothes clean and climbed into bed, I hadn't noticed any in the bed.

What were the odds that the men of the Black Tower liked to freshen their sheets with petals?

More footsteps hurried past my door, reminding me that I needed to get something to eat before reporting to the stablemaster — and that I hadn't eaten dinner last night — *and* that I didn't have a lock on my door. Meaning I should never sleep naked again. I had no idea if those higher up the ranks like Grefin barged in on the sacrifices or not, and I should have thought of that last night when I'd gone to bed.

Except I hadn't had anything else to wear and I hadn't wanted to go to bed in wet or blood-encrusted clothes.

And that was no excuse. It didn't matter what happened, I couldn't let my guard down. Sure, eventually I'd be found out. I wasn't foolish enough to think I could keep up the act forever. But I was damned well going to make sure that didn't happen until Sawyer was at least out of the Five Great Kingdoms.

I grabbed the strips from my ruined dress to flatten my breasts, but the bruise from Edred's beating now covered most of my chest, making me pause. The dark red stain under my skin hurt every time I drew breath and hurt even more when I brushed it with my fingers.

Swell. The next few days weren't going to be fun, but there wasn't anything I could do about it. I couldn't forego my bindings and look like a girl, but I also needed to figure out how to move without looking like I was in pain so I wouldn't get sent to whatever infirmary the Black Guard had — and with my luck, given that they had water in each room, a bathhouse, and laundry bins, they probably had an infirmary with a fae doctor who'd know the second he touched me that I was a girl.

I sucked in a deep breath to steady my nerves then wrapped the strips as tight as I could bear, then I gingerly pulled on the rest of my clothes.

My jerkin was still slightly damp and had a rip in the back where the shadow monster's claws had caught me, and I hadn't managed to completely remove the bloodstains on it or my shirt, but there wasn't anything I could do about it. And really, I was just grateful I'd managed to get through the fight with stained clothes and a headache from where I'd bumped my head.

I shoved my feet into Sawyer's old boots and then reached for the door. My hand trembled and I couldn't make myself open it.

This was the real test. Last night it had been dark, there hadn't been many men around, and those who had been around had been distracted — which had to be why Talon hadn't noticed the truth about me.

And while it didn't look like it was light out yet, I doubted that would last long. With my clothes more or less cleaned up, the men of the Black Tower would now be able to get a good look at me, and without a doubt they were going to know the truth the moment they saw me.

Great Father, I don't know if I can do this.

The vision of the mist swirling around Sawyer's body, his dead eyes staring at nothing, shuddered through me.

Except I had to do this. I *could* do it.

Just long enough for him to escape.

Keep your head down, take whatever punishment Lord Commander Rider gives you—

My thoughts stuttered at that. Was his name actually Rider or had I made that up in my dream as well? Although Talon had mentioned a Rider being upset and Grefin had referred to Lord Rider not liking lazy men so that had to be the Lord Commander's name.

And now I was just stalling.

Fighting not to grit my teeth so I wouldn't look like there was anything wrong with me, I eased my door open. A man in the Guards' black uniform hurried past without giving me a second look and headed down the hall where the men in the lounge had stared at me last night, while another man — a heavily muscled fae man, bulkier than any of the fae I'd seen so far — came out of the stairwell beside my room with a towel wrapped around his hips. His gaze swept over me and I took a hesitant step back under his scrutiny.

"Thought there'd be more to you," he said, his voice gruff before striding to a door halfway down the hall and stepping inside.

More to me? Swell. It looked like people were already talking about me which was only going to make staying unnoticed more difficult. With luck, my next few days would be uneventful or one of the other sacrifices would be more interesting and they'd soon forget about me.

Two more men, fully dressed, strode past me and headed down the hall the first man had gone. Grefin had said to follow everyone else to get to the morning meal so I followed them, keeping a good distance back so they wouldn't notice me.

They strode past the sitting area but instead of turning down the hall to the stairs where I'd first entered the building, they kept going straight.

This hall had a dozen doors on each side, all close together suggesting that they were more individual rooms for the guards, and ended in a set of heavy wooden doors straight ahead and a smaller plain door on the left.

The men took the smaller door, which opened into a stairwell, and I followed, heading down to the ground floor and stepping out another plain door into a wide hall with even more men, all heading toward an open set of enormous double doors.

Beyond, I could hear the roar of voices. It sounded like the great hall in Herstind Keep during the evening meal when most of Edred's men gathered to eat and drink and look at me with the same kind of hunger the men in my dream had given me.

Except this wasn't Herstind and these men didn't know I was a girl. *Please don't let them know.*

A big burly human brushed past me, and I fell into step behind him, hoping to use him as a shield and hide from too many curious eyes. Inside was indeed like the great hall in Herstind.

The room was enormous, towering at least two-stories high. To my right at the far end was another set of large double doors with an enormous window above them filled with expensive glass that was clearer than any glass I'd seen before.

Weak light, the kind that came as dawn was just starting to lighten the sky shone through the window as well as from numerous windows on both sides of the walls. The rest of the room's illumination came from the strange, steady glow of fae lights in four enormous chandeliers hanging overhead and the flickering light from the fire in two large hearths on either side of the room.

Long tables and benches had been placed in orderly rows, but unlike Herstind, there wasn't a dais at the front or a head table of any kind, suggesting the Lord Commander didn't eat with his men.

There also weren't any servants serving food. Which made sense since women weren't a part of the Black Guard and, according to Grefin, rank and position didn't mean anything in the Tower. Instead, the men lined up along the wall closest to the entrance where I'd entered, walked through a door at the back of the room, likely into the kitchen, and walked out of a door on the other side with a tray filled with food.

The large man I was hiding behind headed straight into the line and I hurried to stay in his shadow. Another human stepped up behind me. He was just as big and burly as the man in front. In fact, it seemed all the men in the Tower were big, which I knew wasn't true. There were a few humans closer to my height. But they were all broader and more muscular, because of course they were men and had filled out from all the weapons training they'd done.

"They haven't given you your gear yet?" the man behind me asked.

I didn't know if he was talking to me or not and I wasn't going to look back and make eye contact to find out.

"Probably don't have anything his size," another guy behind me chuckled.

Guess he had been talking to me.

The guy in front of me turned, glanced down then looked at the men behind me. "The novices don't have to arrive until noon. They're probably waiting for everyone to assemble before bothering the quartermaster."

"I'd still be surprised if he has anything in his size," laughing guy said. "You sure you're actually a man?"

My pulse froze. Had I been discovered already?

"He's here so his name was drawn," the man in front of me replied with a shrug and he step through the doorway into the kitchen. "Must mean he's a man."

He picked up a tray on a counter and set a bowl of porridge on it then took a few more steps along the counter giving me my first full view of the kitchen.

It was larger than the kitchen in Herstind, but then it had to feed more than quadruple the number of men. Two large cooking fires took up half of the back wall. One had a spit with a large chunk of meat on it being periodically turned by a man in black guard clothes and armor, and the other had half a dozen large pots hanging over it. More men dressed in guardsmen's clothing — complete with armor and weapons — stood at counters preparing food or washing dishes, while the men in the line loaded their trays with porridge and bread and bacon and—

Great Father! Was that fruit? Apples and grapes and even oranges from the Southern Isles.

Men seemed to take as much or as little as they wanted and no one stopped them. If a platter or bowl was empty, someone in the kitchen replaced it, and if someone didn't notice and the man in line wanted it, he asked for it and was given it without argument or complaint.

I took a bowl of porridge, a small roll, and a precious orange, feeling a little like I was stealing, then found myself at the other door staring into the great hall at the sea of black-armored men devouring their morning meal.

The men closest to me gave me a terse glance. One of them huffed like the fae man in the towel and they returned to their conversation.

The man who'd been in line behind me, brushed past me and I drew closer to the wall to get out of the way while I figured out what to do. There weren't any empty tables or even large spaces between obvious social groups, and I didn't want to plop myself down and join any of them since I had no idea what kind of reception I'd receive. Not to mention the whole point was to keep my head down and not draw unwanted attention.

"You're never going to get that eaten before the second bell if you don't sit down," Talon's sensual tenor said close to my ear, sending a shiver of desire rushing down my spine which quickly mixed with the fear of being discovered and being too close to him and—

He pressed a hand between my shoulder blades, making the shiver melt into aching need, and nudged me between the closest row of tables before I could step away, leading me to a seat beside Grefin, who rolled his eyes at me.

"Speaking of the idiot," he sighed, but he shifted to the side to give me more space on the bench.

CHAPTER 26

Sage

T<small>ALON TOOK MY TRAY</small>, set it on the table before I could apologize and leave, nudged me down on the bench then sat on my other side, boxing me in between him and Grefin.

"You know what he did?" Grefin asked, looking past me at Talon.

"I can't believe he killed a shadow hound," the fae man sitting across from Grefin said.

He was handsome, like all the fae I'd seen, with short black hair and sapphire eyes, but thinner. I had no doubt he was strong and fast, but he was built for quick precision attacks, the kind of fighting I needed to strive for when in battle because neither of us would win a fight if it came down to wrestling... well, he'd win against me and maybe half of the humans here, but no one else.

"I don't believe it," another fae said as he approached, sweeping an appraising gaze over me that made me want to shrink in on myself. He was big, almost twice as broad as the thin fae, with heavy, bulky muscles that were obvious even fully clothed in his Black Guard gear. "He's too small."

He set his tray on the table beside the thin fae's then sat on the bench and captured the thin fae's lips in a powerful kiss that no one else reacted to. I dropped my gaze to my porridge in an attempt to hide my shock. I'd only ever seen men kissing each other in my dream last night, and while Talon had said there were fae mates among the Guard, I didn't think they'd be so open about it.

Unless, of course, that was the point: to see how the new sacrifice would react to them.

"And yet Rider says he did," Talon said, making me hyperaware of him right beside me, his arm mere inches from mine.

My attention jumped to him of its own volition, drawn to him like it had been drawn to Quill yesterday when he'd delivered Sawyer's summons.

Talon was just as stunning as he'd been last night, the Black Guardsmen uniform a stark contrast to his long white hair that shimmered as if some strands were real silver. Four braids at each temple still held his hair back from his face, and light flickered off the earring decorating one of his delicately pointed ears.

Then the memory of his naked body flooded me, reigniting the slick ache between my thighs. I yanked my gaze back to my porridge, my ears burning with embarrassment, praying he hadn't noticed. Maybe he'd sat me here knowing the two across from me were in an intimate relationship. Was this his way of showing me my desires for men weren't going to get me ridiculed or punished like it would in the human realm... if I'd actually been a man?

"You're missing the point," Grefin groaned. "He used the ring after dark which was how he ended up in that mess in the first place."

Aaaaand... it looked like I was never going to live that down. Not with Grefin at least, and if the other guardsmen felt the way he did, not with the rest of the Guard, either.

I shoveled a spoonful of porridge into my mouth, surprised — and yet with everything I'd seen so far, not that surprised — that it was good: creamy and nutty and slightly sweet. Best not to say anything. Just let them think I was an idiot, no matter how much it stung.

"Really?" the large fae asked, sounding genuinely surprised. "I thought all humans knew not to use the ring in the Gray after dark."

"They're supposed to," another man said as he joined the group. He was human with a shaved head and a deeply tanned complexion like Edred and probably around the same age but without the cruel gleam in his pale eyes. He sat on the other side of the large fae and used the edge of his piece of bread to scoop up his porridge instead of a spoon. "You turn sixteen, your name goes in the lottery, and the village priest tells you everything you need to know."

"Is that how it worked for you?" the thin fae asked him.

"Yeah, but I had two older brothers and already knew everything before the priest visited our house," the man replied.

"So, the only way this idiot didn't know was if he thought he was too noble to be selected and didn't pay attention," Grefin said around a mouthful of bread.

The other human's gaze jerked up to me. "You're a noble?"

Damn, was that going to be another detail that drew attention to me?

"Unless—" The thin fae frowned. "What's your name?"

"Sawyer," I replied, remembering to keep my voice gruff.

"I'm Kit. This is my mate Payne and our teammate, Lewin," Kit said. "And Sawyer might not know if he doesn't have any older brothers and hadn't talked to the priest yet," he said to Grefin.

Grefin huffed. "The priests talk to everyone on their sixteenth birthday."

Except the priest wouldn't have talked with Sawyer because he wasn't sixteen and he was the heir to Herstind March.

But I couldn't draw attention to that, either.

Even if there was a chance that I could convince the Lord Commander that Sawyer didn't belong here, I couldn't take it. Everyone would get stuck on the fact that I was a girl and that I didn't belong and that Sawyer had shirked his duty, and I couldn't risk them hauling him back to the Gray and having the premonition of his death come true.

"I didn't realize it got dark in the Gray earlier than elsewhere," I said. "I won't make that mistake again." Not that I was ever going to be allowed to leave the Gray... until they discovered the truth. Then I doubted I'd be free to go anywhere, let alone return here. Not that I'd want to.

And if I was smart, I'd get away from these men before they asked more questions or looked at me more closely.

"I've got chores." I grabbed my tray but had no idea where to go or what to do with it.

"You have a bit of time before the second bell," Talon said, drawing my attention again, capturing me in his mesmerizing swirling gaze.

My breath caught in my throat and the need he'd awaken, that I'd explored in my dream but hadn't come close to satisfying, swelled hot and slick between my thighs.

Shadows he was beautiful! And I knew what he looked like naked—

And I had to remember no matter how nice he was to me, I couldn't trust him. I couldn't trust anyone. Anyone of them could turn on me as easily as Talon had in my dream and I couldn't ever let myself forget that.

CHAPTER 27

Sage

"I'VE ALREADY MADE a bad impression on the Lord Commander," I said, making Grefin huff and Talon shoot him a dark look. "I, ah..."

As if speaking of him made him appear, the Lord Commander strode through the doorway across from me, looking just as gruff and beautiful and imposing as he had been last night in the bailey when he'd been mad at me.

His dark hair — which was indeed black, not brown, with a silver streak at his left temple — was half down, reaching his shoulders, and half pulled back in a topknot to keep it out of his face, and he still wore all his sheathed weapons as if he was always ready for battle—

And now that I thought about it, every man I'd seen had been armed with at least a sword and dagger, even those working in the kitchen. Payne even had two swords and the man on the bench behind him had a large ax strapped to his back. Edred and Sawyer had only worn their weapons inside for ceremonies, and Edred's men had only had weapons when they were on guard duty or hunting brigands.

The Lord Commander's dark gaze landed on me and his scowl deepened.

Yeah, not even a hint of the kindness I'd given him in my dream.

His gaze dipped to the tray in my hands and somehow his expression darkened even more. I had no idea what he was upset about. Probably the orange. Troublemakers probably didn't get delicacies like oranges, and I should have known not to take one.

He started striding toward me. And it was clear he was headed for me because his silver gaze bored into me the entire time. Everything within me screamed to flee. There was an intensity to his gaze that declared him a predator and me his prey.

But I knew escape wasn't an option. There was nowhere to go and with no escape, fleeing would only make my punishment worse. It certainly had with Edred.

Would he beat me like Edred did? Perhaps going to the stables at the second bell had been a trap and he was going to tell me I should have gone at the first bell. Edred liked to change the rules as well.

I tightened my grip on my tray, trying to hide my trembling hands. I couldn't look weak. I couldn't make anyone question my masculinity.

He stormed closer and I instinctually dropped my gaze then remembered what Talon had said. A Guardsman didn't look down for anyone, not even the Lord Commander.

I yanked my gaze up and met the Lord Commander's eyes head on. My stomach churned with the fear of reprisal, but if I was a man and if I was going to be a Guardsman, I needed to accept that looking up wasn't necessarily an act of defiance that needed to be punished. It was just how it was supposed to be. Man to man. Guardsman to commander.

"Kit," the Lord Commander growled, his attention jumping to the skinny fae. "Your team's assignment has changed. Last night's hunting teams said there was increased activity near the gates so I'm adding your team to the patrols this morning."

"You're just doing that because the quartermaster doesn't want me mending clothes anymore," Payne drawled, his tone overly familiar, as if the Lord Commander wasn't the Lord Commander and just another fae.

Lewin rolled his eyes at him. "No one wants you mending our clothes. That's why you were assigned to an elite team. So, you wouldn't ever be given that chore again. You've been here for nine years and you still can't sew a straight line."

"Do you need me to assign a fourth to your unit," the Lord Commander asked, not acknowledging the banter either negatively or positively.

"Permanently. Please," Lewin begged. "Get us back to full hunting duties."

"You'll have a complete unit soon," Rider replied. "I want to get the novices started on their training first then open up the elite competition."

"Who knows," Talon added. "There might already be a few novices ready to join the elite."

Everyone's eyes slid to me.

"Not if they're all as dumb as this one," Grefin huffed.

"I'll remind you that *this one* has already killed a hound," Talon said.

"No," Rider growled. "*This one* got lucky." He turned his attention back to Kit. "Do you want a fourth?"

"Depends on who you want to give me," Kit replied.

"I'll go," Talon volunteered. "It'll be nice to patrol the Gray again."

Payne snorted. "You have a fucked-up definition of nice."

"And I need you at the main gate watching the novices arrive." The Lord Commander's attention jumped back to me, making me want to curl in on myself and disappear. "I don't want anymore surprises and I want your initial assessment of them before we get them situated."

"Fine," Talon sighed.

"And we really don't need a fourth to patrol around the gate in the day," Kit added.

"All right." The Lord Commander turned on his heel and marched into the kitchen without — thank the Father! — commenting on my orange.

"Well, he's in a bad mood," Payne said.

Grefin shot me a dark look. "Gee, I wonder why."

"I should go," I mumbled.

Lewin gave me an apologetic look then pointed behind me. "There's a bin at the back of the room for your dirty dishes."

"Thanks." I hurried away before anyone else could say anything, set my tray in the bin with the other trays and dirty dishes, and, with my precious orange in hand, went back to the corridor where I'd first entered.

I hadn't seen anyone come or go from the main doors in the great hall and didn't want to make a scene by leaving that way. It was bad enough half of the men in the room were staring at me and this time I knew it had everything to do with me — my size and the fact that I was the idiot who'd used the ring after dark last night — since I was no longer covered in shadow blood.

I guessed that the first floor of the barracks was identical to the third floor and if I went straight instead of going back up the stairs I'd taken to get to the great hall, I'd find another hall that led to that first door Grefin had taken me to when we'd entered the building last night.

I was right, and I hurried outside into a cramped area between the three-story barracks and a one-story section of the building. Mist curled thick around my feet and ankles and the air was damp and chilly. Above, the sky was dull and overcast, and while it didn't look like it was going to rain, it also didn't look like the sun was going to come out anytime soon.

On the other side of the one-story section of the main building lay the bailey. It was easily three times the size of Herstind castle's bailey enclosed by tall walls that I had no doubt were thicker than the ones surrounding Herstind castle.

Ahead of me, the stables and its outbuildings took up the right wall almost from the edge of the barracks all the way to the main gate, while to the left was a large section jutting off the main building, the strange building I'd noticed last night that was made of the semi-opaque material, and another large building that I had no idea what it was.

A few men sparred near the building that I had no idea what it was, while four more walked out of the stables with their riding tack and headed to one of the outbuildings close to me. One of them, a human with a medium sized build and short brown hair noticed me and said something to the guy beside him and then all four of them — two humans and two fae — were staring at me. They all looked tired and were splattered with shadow blood and one of the humans had a cut on his cheek.

"If you're going to be stupid enough to draw their attention by using the ring after dark, at least be good enough to kill more than just one of them," one of the fae said as they entered the outbuilding.

"I'm just impressed you managed to kill one of them at all," a familiar voice said from behind me, and I turned to see Kit coming around the edge of the building.

"I got lucky." Which was an understatement. "Are you following me to make sure I don't get into anymore trouble?"

"Talon was worried you didn't get enough to eat." Kit held out a slice of bread folded into a sandwich with cheese and bacon in the middle.

I took it, not wanting to argue with him and because I was still a little hungry since I'd only eaten part of my roll and half of my porridge before the Lord Commander had shown up.

"Thanks," I said, "but Talon doesn't have to concern himself with me." And neither did anyone else. In fact, the fewer people who noticed me, the better.

Payne and Lewin strode around the edge of the building toward us, the large fae flashing me a wide grin.

"See you when the fourth bell rings, novice," he said. He wrapped an arm across Kit's shoulders without losing a step and they headed to the same outbuilding the other men had gone into.

Swell. They weren't going to ignore me and that would just draw even more attention.

CHAPTER 28
Sage

I ATE THE HALF SANDWICH, then peeled and ate my orange. The first four men left the outbuilding and returned to the barracks, while Kit and his team picked up their riding gear, headed into the stables, and returned to the bailey a few minutes later with their horses saddled and ready to go.

Payne swung up into his saddle with the powerful grace only a fae could have, gave me a wave as the others mounted, then all three of them rode out of the bailey.

I finished my orange, shoved the peels into my pocket — I'd add them to the manure pile when I had a chance — and crossed the bailey to the stables.

The castle's bell rang twice just as I was stepping inside the large, dusty building filled with the pungent, musty scent of hay and horse and urine and shit. A middle-aged human with a sword at his hip, a robust figure, and thinning hair looked up from whatever he'd been doing a few stalls down and frowned at me.

"So, you're the novice," he said, his tone dry.

Swell. Another admirer.

Another man, about my age — my real age of almost twenty, not the age I was pretending to be — hurried through the stable doors and stopped beside me. He too was armed, and he gave me a quick glance before turning his attention to the middle-aged man.

"I'm the stablemaster, Kasen," the middle-aged man said. "Today you're mine until the fourth bell and then for half of the shift after the eighth bell. Have you mucked out a stall before?"

"I haven't," I admitted. No point in claiming to know something when I didn't since I wasn't here to impress anyone.

"He's a noble," the new guy snickered. "Probably hasn't had a hard day of work in his life."

Which wasn't at all true. I'd spent a lot of time hauling water up stairs for Edred and his new wife's baths among other things, but I'd never been given stable work.

In fact, shortly after my mother had died, Edred had stopped my riding lessons, and I could only assume it was an effort to limit my knowledge of horses so it would be harder for me to run away.

"Well, he's not a noble anymore," Kasen said.

"Owun, get him started while I start moving the horses to the pasture. Once you've gotten him going, help me with the rest."

Owun gave a tight nod and headed to an area with shovels, brooms, wheelbarrows, buckets, rags, brushes, and a larger version of the pump and basin in my room. He put a shovel into one of the wheelbarrows and wheeled it down the wide aisle between the stalls.

I followed him as dozens of sets of large dark eyes followed us. Horses huffed and whickered and shifted and stomped. Some didn't seem to notice us, while others stretched their heads over the doors, looking for attention. Owun ignored all of them and stopped at a stall that didn't have a horse in it and swung open the door.

"Shovel everything into the wheelbarrow." He held the shovel out to me. "The manure pile is outside the Tower, so when the wheelbarrow is full, follow me or Kasen out the pasture gate and we'll point you in the right direction. Repeat until all the stalls have been shoveled out."

"Got it." I didn't know if there was more to it. At some point we'd have to lay fresh hay, but I wasn't sure if there were anymore steps between shoveling out the spoiled hay and adding the clean stuff, but I was sure Owun would tell me when the time came.

I took the shovel and got to work, trying to ignore the pain in my chest every time I moved, while Owun and Kasen came and went, leading a couple horses at a time out the stable door. The wheelbarrow quickly filled, and I wheeled it to the stable's entrance where Kasen led two horses and me across the bailey and out a narrow archway in the thick outer wall near that building that I had no idea what it was.

Beyond the wall lay a rocky, jagged gray landscape swathed in mist. It reminded me a bit of the wastelands at the edge of Herstind March with scraggly trees and tough weeds, but here was sharper and more dangerous looking.

Ahead lay a field of dark green grass that didn't fit with the rest of the barren landscape where some of the horses were already grazing, and to my right was a squat building with smoke curling from half a dozen chimneys and dozens of empty laundry lines nearby waiting for the day's clean wet laundry.

Beyond that was an enormous area for weapons training. Men were stretching and warming up, while others had already started practice bouts or had lined up in front of archery targets. They laughed and jostled and called to each other with a familiarity and joy I hadn't expected of the Black Guard, sending an unexpected pang of jealousy through me.

They had a comradery I couldn't let myself have with them and one I'd never had with anyone except Sawyer. Lord Quill had been right when he'd said that Sawyer was going to gain three hundred brothers. I was sure that like all families not everyone got along, but I could tell from looking at the men on the practice grounds that many of them did. They needed to rely on each other to stay alive and they couldn't completely do that without first building trust between them.

Which was why using the ring after dark and endangering the lives of whoever had come to save me pissed off most of the men I'd met. I'd proven just by showing up that I couldn't be trusted not to get them into a situation that put them in danger.

Kasen pointed me to the manure pile, which lay down a narrow path and past the practice area. Beyond it I could see the top of the fae ring, easily three or four hundred yards away, and another, wider path leading away from the pile toward the ring.

I dumped my load then headed back to the stables to repeat the process, shoveling, wheeling, returning. The stables were large, so I tried to pace myself, but the ache in my chest continued to grow and I knew that it was going to be difficult to move, let alone breathe, before my first shift in the stables was even done.

After probably about two hours of shoveling, Owun handed me a bucket of soapy water and a scrub brush and pointed me to the first stall I'd cleaned out.

"Give it a good scrub," he said with a satisfied gleam in his eyes, but the gleam vanished when I went into the first stall and got to work scrubbing the stone floor without complaint.

I fought back my own satisfied gleam, knowing I disappointed him by not reacting like a spoiled nobleman. Complaining only drew attention to myself and hopefully, by not saying anything and just doing my job, everyone would forget about me. I'd just be an unmemorable new member of the Guard, nothing more.

Which really wasn't that different from the life I'd left. Sure, I'd been a nobleman's daughter, but I'd always had to do what I was told and with Edred that had been scrubbing floors and hauling water and doing laundry with the other servants. Why pay for a servant when you had someone who could do it for free? It didn't matter that Herstind Keep's servants weren't paid very well. They'd still been paid. I hadn't been.

I suppose there'd been hope that my life would have gotten easier once Edred had finally shipped me off to a husband. But there'd been no guarantee of that, and I suspected anyone Edred liked as a husband for me had a similar disposition and wouldn't have treated me any better. And really, even if he treated me better, he still wouldn't have been able to give me what I wanted: the chance to be my own person and to have the skill to protect the people I cared about.

Except that wasn't *all* I wanted.

A whisper of achy need warmed my core despite the fact that my nose was far too close to a sticky pool of horse piss and my chest hurt.

I wanted to be desired and loved. I didn't want to be with a man to make Edred or any other man happy. I wanted to be with a man to make *me* happy and have a man desire me for me. That was what my dream had really been about. Even if I hadn't looked like me, I still knew that was what it had been about.

I scrubbed my way to the stall door, my thoughts wandering back to the dream and how that man had worked magic with his mouth. I'd never felt anything like that before and had no idea how I'd managed to dream about it.

"Hey," a lilting masculine voice said, startling me from my daydreaming.

I glanced out the stall door to see another gorgeous fae with flawless dark skin standing a few stalls down cooing to a white and gray dappled horse that the stablemaster and Owun had strangely left in his stall.

"How's he looking?" another, just as beautiful fae with long light brown hair, asked, heading to another horse that had also been left behind.

"Flint did a good job. Can hardly tell that hound got him across the nose three nights ago," the other fae replied and stepped into the stall and started saddling the horse.

I turned my attention back to the final few feet of

stall floor left to scrub. They hadn't noticed me and maybe if I kept my head down, they wouldn't. I didn't want a repeat of the snide comments or even the dirty looks that I'd gotten in the great hall.

"So," the first fae said, "did you go to the Garden last night? I heard there was a new arrival."

Hunh, new arrival? That sounded familiar. Wasn't that what the men in my dream had called me? What a funny coincidence that these fae would use the same words the fae in my dream had.

"I didn't see her," the other fae replied, "but my cousin did. Said she had all her marks and stunning dark red hair."

My thoughts tripped on that. I couldn't have heard that right. *I'd* had dark red hair in my dream, too. What were the odds that they'd not only mention a new arrival but one with the same hair color?

"Red hair?" the first fae said. "Then she's definitely new. There isn't an unmated woman with red hair right now. This could be your chance."

"I doubt it."

"Why not?" the first fae asked. "You have magic. You won't know unless you try."

"I barely have magic," the other fae replied. "But Wells, Crane, and Pike found her first and Rider sent them packing."

"Rider scared away the most eligible bachelors in the Garden? He hasn't done that..."

"He's only ever done that for his sister."

A chill swept through me. The Lord Commander actually had a sister. And they knew that he'd told those men to go away.

"If he's finally decided to put himself in the running for a mate, I'm not going anywhere near her," the second fae said. "He's more powerful than me and I bet he'll be worse than Blaze who almost killed two of Lark's suitors until the Goddess bonded him to her."

"Of course, none of those suitors turned out to be her other mates," the first fae replied, "so his instincts were right on that."

"Still not going to court this new woman until I know that Rider isn't going to rip out my throat."

My thoughts spun. How could they have possibly known what I'd dreamed last night?

CHAPTER 29
Sage

THE ONLY WAY those fae could have known what I'd dreamed last night was if they'd used magic. But then if they had, surely they'd have commented on the fact that I'd dreamed about having a strange man make me come with his mouth.

No, all they knew was what everyone in that court-yard had seen: those three men leading me up from the pond, me bumping into the Lord Commander, and him telling them to leave me alone.

So, if they knew that—

If that had actually been real—

I'd woken with a pink flower in my hand—

It had to have been real.

There was no other logical explanation. I had no idea how I'd gotten there or how I'd been a fae when I really was a human but—

Oh, Great Father!

I'd let that man touch me— *told* him to touch me and he'd—

My breath picked up and heat seared over my cheeks and forehead and down my neck. The reason I'd been able to dream about how it felt to come with a man's mouth on me was because I hadn't dreamed it at all.

I'd let a complete stranger give me the most amazing sensations I'd ever felt, and I didn't even know his name and hadn't even seen his face. Which meant I had no idea who to avoid if I ended up in that garden again... or if he was here at the Black Tower.

Shadows, would he recognize me? I'd had long hair and pointed ears and fae-colored eyes and those marks, but I'd still mostly looked like me.

If he was in the Tower and did recognize me, I could only pray he'd think I resembled the woman he'd met last night and wasn't actually that woman, since I was supposed to be a human boy. *Oh, please.*

I sat there, my thoughts whirling, unable to focus on anything. I heard the men lead their horses out of the stables then Owun return with the wheelbarrow.

I'd let that man—

And it had been wonderful.

Was that what sex with all fae men was like?

He hadn't even used his cock and it had been so much better than my time with Royston. In fact, he hadn't even come himself. Was he angry about that? I wasn't sure what had happened after I'd come. Had I blacked out and he'd gotten satisfaction or had I... I had no idea. I didn't understand how I'd gone to sleep in the Black Tower with short hair and woken in that garden with long hair and pointy ears.

Except I did. The Lord Commander had said I looked stunned from manifesting. So, I had to have been manifesting. But I had no idea what that was or how I'd done it.

"You can scrub faster than that," Owun said behind me, making me jump. My elbow hit the bucket, knocking it over and spilling water across the stone floor. "And now you've got to wipe that up or it'll never dry in time. There are rags with the buckets and brooms," he sneered, and he strode away.

I grabbed a handful of rags and returned to the stall, my thoughts still spinning around and around and around. It didn't make sense. Maybe it was because of the fae magic binding me to the Tower. Maybe all of the men here woke in that garden looking like fae.

If that was the case, I wished Grefin had given me a warning before I'd gone to bed last night.

Of course, he'd gotten a good laugh out of showing me the pump and basin. I bet he got another good laugh over seeing the novices stunned from manifesting in that garden.

Except if he had, wouldn't he have made fun of me this morning? Even if he hadn't seen me or realized I was the *new arrival* he would have assumed I'd have gone to sleep, woken in the garden, and been confused.

I cleaned up the mess I made, added more soapy water to my bucket, and moved on to the next stall. I scrubbed, unable to stop my mind from spinning while flashes of embarrassment swept through me in waves. Hot and red, fine and frustrated, then hot and red again... and also a little achy with need then sad with regret.

I now knew that sex was more than what I'd first thought, and the odds weren't good that I was ever going to have it again.

Which was probably the cruelest part of what had happened last night. I couldn't very well seek out that fantasy man and have sex with him again, could I? I didn't know his name, didn't know what he looked like, and with my luck, I'd never manifest again.

And really, I needed to focus on being a man, not a woman in lust. I could never forget my reason for being here.

True to his word, Payne, along with Kit and Lewin, led their horses into the stables and a few moments later the Tower's bell rang four times. The stablemaster dismissed me and I headed back to my room to clean up, but Kit and the others fell into step beside me.

"You're eating the midday meal with us," Kit said, his tone making it clear that it wasn't a request.

Lewin scrunched his nose in disgust. "But clean up first."

"Don't forget to wear whatever weapons you have. Guardsmen are always armed, and the quartermaster will want to see what you've got before he assigns you anything," Payne added.

I headed to my room and they presumably to theirs and cleaned up as best I could. My chest throbbed, but I retied the strips flattening my breasts to ensure they wouldn't slip with whatever I was going to have to do after the midday meal — and I could only pray the quartermaster wouldn't ask me to strip so he could measure me for my new clothes. As a woman, I'd needed to strip for the most expensive dresses that I'd left behind in Herstind, but not for my other dresses, and as far as I knew, Sawyer had only ever had to take off his jerkin to be measured for new outfits.

The midday meal was like the morning meal. Men lined up at the one door to the kitchen, took what they wanted from what was offered, then exited through the other door. There was a hearty stew with potatoes and turnips and meat, bacon probably left over from the morning meal, bread, cheese, vegetables, and more fruit.

I took a modest helping of stew, some bread, and another orange. The one this morning had been so good, sweet and tart and juicy, and if they were going to have oranges available at every meal, I was going to take one at every meal, at least until they learned I was a girl. Then I was pretty sure there'd be no more oranges.

Kit waved me down when I exited the kitchen and I took the empty seat beside Lewin, my insides churning. I didn't like that they were paying attention to me, but I knew if I rejected their offer to eat with them that would only draw more attention.

As it was, even more of the men around me gave me dirty or dismissive looks, and I knew the tale of me coming through the ring after dark had now made its way through the entire guard. Everyone knew I was *that* novice and from their expressions they were now falling into two camps: that I was a dangerous troublemaker or that I was a dangerous idiot.

"Another orange, hunh?" Kit said, digging into his stew.

"I thought noblemen got oranges whenever they wanted," Lewin added, reaching for the orange, but I snatched it away before he could take it, making Payne snort a harsh laugh.

"Not all nobles are as privileged as those in the capital," I said, holding the orange possessively close to my chest.

"And the runt here had to have been the bottom of his pile of nobles," Grefin said, sliding into the seat beside Kit. "He kept 'my lording' me and couldn't look past his feet last night. If they had oranges, I doubt they'd have given him any." He huffed at me. "Probably didn't feed you enough, either. That's why you're so small."

"Then we should fix that," Payne said, ripping his chunk of bread in half and setting a piece on my tray.

"Bad idea," Lewin said, snatching the bread and taking a bite. "He's got assessment this afternoon. We don't want him puking on the course or worse on Rider when he's sparring with him."

"You're right. I should save that for when I'm around to watch him puke on Rider," Payne said with a laugh.

"And then Rider will stick us on the wall nightshift and we'll be too tired to do anything else," Kit shot back.

Payne turned a heated gaze to Kit. "Then I guess we'll just have to get in as much... *anything else* as possible this rotation before Rider changes our shift."

"You're already getting in a lot of *anything else* already," Lewin groaned with a smile.

Payne flashed him a wicked grin. "You can never get enough."

"I'm going to need to spend time in the library tonight, aren't I?" Lewin said. "Oh, the newly mated. Can't keep their hands off of each other."

"Don't worry," Kit said. "We'll take it to the Garden, tonight."

My pulse picked up and I fought not to stare at him. He'd brought up the Garden. Now was my chance to ask about it and maybe I'd be able to figure out why I'd manifested there last night... and how I'd manifested at all for that matter.

CHAPTER 30
Sage

"The Garden?" I asked, trying not to look too eager for his answer even though my pulse pounded so hard I was sure Lewin could hear it.

"It's a fae thing," Grefin said dismissively.

"It's not *just* a fae thing." Payne shot Grefin a frustrated glare.

"It's our everything," Kit said. "It's the most sacred place in our realm, the heart of our people and our goddess. We go there for our most sacred rituals, but also to find mates and to mate. Because any adult can go to the Garden physically but also spiritually, it's also become a place to be social. We could be scattered among the two realms, but we can still close our eyes and manifest our spirits in the Garden."

"Have you seen it?" I asked Lewin who snorted and ended up choking on his ale.

"No," he sputtered between coughs. "Humans aren't allowed. Even if you go to the fae realm, the Garden's magic won't let a human inside."

"Ever?" Well, there went my theory that everyone in the Guard ended up in that garden because of the fae magic binding us to the Tower. Still, there had to be a time when a human had gone there.

"Jeez, that's what he said." Grefin rolled his eyes at me as if I'd just confirmed to him how stupid I really was. "I hope you're at lease half decent with a sword because teaching you is going to be tedious."

He drained his ale in one long gulp then picked up his tray and headed to the back of the hall to get rid of his dirty dishes.

"He'll warm up to you," Kit said, digging in to his stew.

"Unless, of course, you really are terrible with a sword," Payne added.

Swell. I didn't think my swordsmanship was terrible, but I also wasn't strong compared to everyone else here. And while I was fast, it only took one good strike from an opponent to lose a bout. That and my whole body was starting to hurt from the work I'd done that morning, so I had no doubt I wasn't going to be able to do my best that afternoon and that was just going to prove to Grefin how hopeless I was.

"Cheer up," Lewin said. "We don't think you're stupid."

"Yeah." Payne ripped off another chunk of bread and set it on my tray to replace the piece Lewin had stolen. "Humans can't go to the Garden, so most humans don't know about it. The only reason the human Guardsmen know is because half of the Guard is fae and at least half of us are hoping to be bound to a female mate."

Except I'd been there.

It must have been a mistake. The fae magic binding me to the Tower had still been new and a little hot in my arm when I'd gone to sleep. It had to have somehow mixed with my strange ability to have premonitions and I'd ended up there last night.

But now that the burn was gone — I hadn't even noticed it waking up in the morning — I'd be fine. When I went to bed tonight, I'd stay in my bed and I wouldn't have to worry about embarrassing myself in front of that mystery man or the Lord Commander or Talon.

"Are you two hoping for a female mate?" I wasn't sure why I asked and as soon as the words slipped out, I realized how rude the question probably was.

"No," Payne said unoffended as he glanced at Kit, his amethyst eyes filled with a fierce love that warmed my heart while also making me a little jealous. He was truly in love with Kit. The kind of love talked about in the minstrels' tales. The kind of love that as a noblewoman I'd never have. "Even if I had magic and was eligible, I wouldn't."

"I have magic, so I'd have been eligible before we took our vows," Kit said, "but no one's soul, woman's or man's, has ever called to me like Payne's."

"It's all so romantically disgusting," Lewin said, his tone playful, clearly not upset that his teammates were in a relationship. "Fae in love are the worst."

Lewin teased Kit and Payne a bit more about being too sappy for Guardsmen then the conversation shifted to talk about the increased number of shadow monsters, especially during the daytime, and how this year was the largest number of novices the Tower had ever seen.

The bell rang five times and Kit, Payne, and Lewin grabbed their dirty trays — Payne grabbing mine as well — and they left me sitting on the bench waiting for my official assessment to begin.

The great hall cleared out and soon there were only five groups sitting at various tables and me. The group closest to me was all fae. There were nine of them, all big, all muscular, all armed, and all looked like they knew what to do with their weapons. They weren't, however, in black, so I could only assume they were the fae novices.

The other four groups consisted of humans of a variety of ages — although none of them looked to be as young as Sawyer — and, from the quality of their

clothes, all walks of life as well. There were twenty —
so twenty-one human sacrifices if I included myself —
and five of them looked just as dangerous and skilled
as the nine fae. They must have been the humans Lord
Quill had mentioned, the ones who saw joining the
Guard as an honor and a duty and prepared for it.

They all had numerous weapons strapped to their
bodies and all looked at the rest of us as if we were
lesser than they were. And in truth we probably were.
They were already warriors. We weren't.

Three of them sat together in their own small
group, and talked quietly amongst themself and I got
the impression they knew each other, while the other
two sat in different groups. The rest of the groups were
a mix of possibly skilled and possibly hopeless men. A
few of them had weapons but mostly didn't.

Two of the humans — a man who looked to be a
little older than the real me, and a boy probably a year
or two younger — were too plump to have been in a
physical profession before their names had been
drawn and were likely going to struggle with whatever
initial training we were going to get. While another
man who looked to be older than everyone else, probably twenty-six, sat at the edge of one of the groups, his
expression desolate. He'd probably thought he'd made
it, probably had a life before his name had been
drawn. There were probably children who were going
to be without a father now.

The Lord Commander, along with Talon and Lord Quill, marched through the same doorway the Lord Commander had come through at the morning meal. They were breathtaking, the most achingly beautiful men in the room and something soft shivered through me.

What was it with the fae men?

No, not all fae. My pulse didn't stutter when Kit or Payne looked at me.

There was something about Lord Quill and Talon — and Lord Rider if I was being honest with myself — that made it hard to look away.

I tried to not stare at them, but just like the last few times I'd run into them, I couldn't seem to help myself. There was something about them, something compelling, and it wasn't just Talon with his magic. All three of them tugged at something within me.

They stopped at the closest — and empty — table and swept their gazes over the room.

"I don't want to yell," The Lord Commander said, pointing to the empty table in front of him even though I was sure he was perfectly capable of yelling.

Everyone got up and moved and the Lord Commander watched us, his gaze appraising, assessing us by how we hurried or didn't hurry to our new seats. And when his gaze fell on me, I could tell by the way his eyes narrowed, that he'd already made up his mind about me and that I was lacking.

CHAPTER 31
Sage

WE ALL SAT on the bench, the nine fae sticking together at the end of our group, their gazes sliding over the humans, assessing us the same way the Lord Commander had and, of course, narrowing when they got to me. I didn't know if they knew what I'd done, but even if they didn't, I was the smallest of the group and looked about as much of a warrior as the two heavyset guys.

The three humans who looked like they knew how to fight sat at the other end of the table, and I took a spot between two men who didn't have weapons but might possibly be able to wield them and behind one of the larger guys, hoping that if the Lord Commander couldn't really see me, he'd stop glaring at me. That and hopefully I'd be able to stop staring at him, Talon, and Lord Quill.

"I'm Lord Commander Rider," he said, shifting so he could look at me. Swell. "You can call me Commander Rider, Lord Rider, or Lord Commander. This is Lord Talon, Captain of the Gold Tower, and Lord Quill, Captain of the White Tower."

"Only call me Lord when we're in the Gold Tower," Lord— or rather *just* Talon said. "I get enough stuffy nobleman talk there. I'd rather not have it here."

The men around me all nodded and some of the tension eased from the group. They still didn't know what to expect, but Talon asking them to be informal with him set a more relaxed tone, and I supposed if you were trying to build a brotherhood with strangers who had no choice being there, being less formal was an immediate way to start building trust. Talon taking away his title also took away a wall between him and the sacrifices and made him seem more approachable.

Lord Rider cleared his throat, drawing our attention back to him. "From this moment forward you're novices in the Black Guard. Who you were before you came to the Gray doesn't matter. Peasant or noble, human or fae, it doesn't matter. If you work hard, you'll be rewarded with better assignments, more lieu time, and extra bits. Slack off or screw up—" His gaze landed on me and his eyes narrowed "—and you'll lose lieu time, get extra duties, and be docked pay."

"We get paid?" The older of the two heavy-set men asked.

"Yes," Lord Talon said. "Ten bits a rotation which can be spent on clothing for your lieu time, things for your room, treats we don't make in the kitchen—"

"Or women," one of the clearly skilled sacrifices said with a big grin, making the nine fae bristle. "My cousin said we take lieu time in Lehyrst and there's a brothel just for us."

"You're correct," Talon said, then he went on to explain how the Black Guard worked.

There were three shifts — which was why the bells came in sets of three. An early shift, where the first two bells were meals and get to work, and a late shift were the second two bells were meal and then get to work. Those shifts consisted of morning and afternoon duties with the evening off, while the third shift was at night where the meal breaks weren't scheduled like they were in the day. You were assigned a shift for a rotation, which consisted of eight to ten days of duties and anywhere from one to three lieu days and then your shift — and hence your duties — changed.

Because we were novices we were on a special shift where we were going to be turned into warriors. Of course, that didn't mean we'd been excluded from chores. Everyone, with the exception of the elite units, was given a chore, from washing clothes, to mending them, to working in the kitchen or cleaning the floors or the stables or the bathhouse.

"You fuck up, you end up mucking stalls or doing

laundry," Rider growled, glaring at me, the look not going unnoticed by the other fae and the three skilled humans, "and you'll make a few senior guardsmen really happy because you'll be taking their shift."

"So do they get the time off?" one of the younger sacrifices asked.

"That or they get a less strenuous duty, like working for the cook, the quartermaster, the seneschal, or the healers," Talon replied.

Lord Rider then went on to explain how everyone had to have a weapon and had to wear it at all times. "The Guard is always ready to defend the Gates against the shadows. If the spell sealing the Shadow Gate ever fails, we may not get a warning and we must always be prepared. Even if you never become a great swordsman and end up mostly in a support role, you must be prepared to fight."

The fae and the five obviously skilled humans all nodded with grim understanding, while the two heavy-set sacrifices and half of the other humans all looked green at the prospect of fighting.

"All right," Lord Rider said. "Now who have we got? Stand when your name is called and speak up if you have a trade or skill that might be useful, combat experience, or magic."

Lord Quill pulled a piece of thin, fae paper from a pocket in his jerkin as if it wasn't an incredibly expensive thing that only the nobles in the capital could

afford and started calling out names. Men acknowledged their names while the rest of us studied each
other. Three of the nine fae said they had magic, which
surprised me since I'd thought all fae had magic. But
then, Payne had mentioned at the midday meal that he
didn't have magic.

The oldest of the sacrifices was a smith, and the
younger of the two heavyset men had been an apprentice chef in Vestas, the largest port city in Erellod.
There was a hunter — he'd come with a long dagger
and a bow and quiver — a few farmers and shop-
keepers and traders, a priest of the Great Father who'd
just taken his vows, and a sailor who looked almost as
distressed as the smith because given the landscape of
the Gray, there wasn't a significant body of water
anywhere nearby.

The five humans who looked like they knew how to
fight did know how to fight. Two of them were from the
armies of two different noble families and the other
three were essentially mercenaries. Essentially because
they were from three of the families that trained their
young men to take positions in the Black Guard, saving
the sons of the most noble families in the Five Great
Kingdoms from becoming sacrifices.

"We can fight with a variety of weapons on foot and
from horseback," Mikel Wild said, gesturing to the
other two men who'd been sitting with him. They were
all big with broad shoulders and muscles honed from

years of weapons training, although none of them were as big as the majority of the fae. "We've also been trained in military tactics and formations and have experience fighting together."

"Have you seen actual combat?" Lord Rider asked.

"Yes," Durand said. He was the smallest of the three which still made him almost a head taller than me with a chest almost twice as broad.

"What about you two?" Lord Rider asked, turning to the two soldiers.

"I was just a grunt," Ambrose said, his build similar to Durand's. "So, formations but not tactics and no experience fighting from horseback."

"Same here," the other soldier replied.

Lord Rider grunted and glanced at Quill who turned his attention to me, his emerald eyes capturing mine for a breathtaking moment.

I tried to meet his gaze and hold it without cringing. The aching need to fall into those bottomless green eyes and never return to the surface battled with the urge to look down and look small twisted my insides. A lady wasn't supposed to draw attention to herself, she was supposed to quietly be ready to please her lord, be graceful and proper and demure at all times. And not hold eye contact with a man, no matter how captivating he was.

"Sawyer Herstind," Lord Quill said, and I stood as a

wave of murmurs swept through the group that made my stomach twist even tighter.

"Herstind March."

"He's a lord."

"Guess he couldn't buy his way out of being a sacrifice."

"Did you hear what he did last night?"

Swell. Somehow some of the novices already knew about my mistake. Of course, the fae were volunteers and probably had friends in the guard already, and the three from families who bred Guardsmen probably had brothers or cousins or some other family member already in the Guard. They'd all taken the midday meal in the great hall and just like I'd been the conversation this morning, I had no doubt I'd been the conversation this afternoon. Hell, even if I did keep my head down, I'd probably still be the conversation for the rest of this rotation.

"I have a bit of experience with a sword," I said, making Mikel snort.

"Look at him," Durand snickered. "He's one of those lords that spent all his time reading. Too good to even learn how to fight."

No, I spent it learning to fight in secret while cleaning floors and lugging water and struggling to learn the things I was supposed to learn like making lace and sewing embroidery and keeping my gaze down.

"Can you even hold a sword long enough to fight with it?" Ambrose asked.

Lord Rider shot him then Durand and Mikel dark glares and they all snapped their mouths shut.

"You're not a lord now," Lord Rider growled at me, "and we'll find out soon enough how much *experience* you have with a sword."

CHAPTER 32
Sage

WITH THAT LORD Rider left and Talon and Lord Quill took us on a tour. We headed out the great hall's main doors and stood in the bailey while Talon pointed to the various buildings. The structure by the pasture gate that I had no idea what it was turned out to be an indoor sparring area for when the weather turned bad, and the small building made from the strange semi-opaque material was a fae greenhouse where the healers grew medicinal herbs.

We then marched down a long hall to the infirmary and were greeted by a fae who wasn't in Guard black and looked identical to the fae with the short brown hair and medium brown skin who'd made love to Lark in my dream last night... the dream that hadn't been a dream.

Talon introduced him, and he said something and

gestured to the infirmary behind him, but I completely missed everything that was said.

Because he was real.

I'd seen him completely naked, his cock hard and ready, his mouth and hands caressing and teasing Lark along with the other men. He'd had his fingers inside her, made her moan with a pleasure that had awakened my own need and made it blossom into a hot, achy throbbing between my thighs. He'd made love to her mouth while another man had licked and sucked her to climax. He'd—

Heat burned my face, and I shifted slightly behind one of the larger fae novices to hide myself from the healer. I didn't think he'd recognize me. Neither Lord Rider, Lord Quill, nor Talon had recognized me as the red-haired woman in the garden, and the healer had been completely focused on Lark. But just looking at him reminded me of what I'd done and felt and craved, and that it had all been real.

Then we were marched to the quartermaster's rooms and my pulse picked up even faster. This was the moment where everything could go terribly wrong and they'd discover the truth.

Talon pointed out the large board on the wall by the quartermaster's door with the Guard's shift assignments and Lord Quill helped those who couldn't read find their name and their assignments for our current rotation. Then one by one we stood in front of the quartermaster who stood beside a wide, tall table.

The quartermaster was a gruff old human with an eyepatch and a thick scar running down the side of his face that twisted his upper right lip into a perpetual sneer. He, too, even though he was well past his prime wore a short sword at his hip and two long daggers at his other hip. He looked at our weapons and either proclaimed them adequate or not before running a quick appraising glance over each of us — not even bothering to measure us — and calling out a number. A guardsman standing by would then take whoever it was into a backroom, and they'd return loaded with clothes and boots and armor and weapons — if weapons were required.

As instructed, I unsheathed Sawyer's—

No, I corrected myself. I guess it was my longsword now not Sawyer's and set it on the table for the quartermaster's inspection. He approved it and approved of my dagger then frowned at me.

"How old are you, boy?" he asked, his voice gruff.

"Sixteen," I lied, both on my real age and Sawyer's.

"So still growing. Good. One," he said to the guardsman beside him. "Use the vambraces to keep your hands clear until you can grow into the shirt and just tuck the pants into the boots." The quartermaster's frown deepened. "Best to keep your own boots. I don't think we have anything small enough."

The guardsman led me into a storeroom with rows and rows of shelves and racks and bins stocked with everything: clothes, boots, belts, towels, blankets, soap, weapons of every kind. He piled two shirts, two pants, a heavy jerkin, and a set of vambraces for my forearms then ushered me back to the front room.

Once everyone had their new clothes and armor, we were led to the barracks, told about the individual rooms, the pump and basin, the bathhouse in the basement, and where the laundry bins were. Then we were assigned rooms and told to change and meet in the bailey ready to have our physical abilities assessed.

I quickly changed into a shirt that was indeed too big, but thankfully didn't show the extra fabric flattening my chest when I had it laced all the way up. The pants were also too big in the legs and in the waist and were only being held up by my sword belt. And, of course, the jerkin was too big, hanging low enough on my hips that it made it a little difficult to draw my sword and dagger, and unfortunately since I needed it to hold my pants up, I couldn't set my sword belt lower on my hips for a smoother draw.

I got more than my fair share of looks and snickers when I hurried out of the barracks and even a huff from the Lord Commander who looked, if it was even possible, less impressed with me than before.

"This your first time not being in anything but the best?" Mikel whispered to me, making Durand and the other *experienced* fighters snicker. "Better get used to it, *my lord*."

Had he not seen my ripped jerkin and soiled shirt and pants when we'd been marching through the castle?

But then he wasn't commenting because he was unobservant. He was hoping to embarrass me, put me in my place, remind me that I no longer had the privilege of being called a lord.

Bad luck for him that Edred had already made my lack of privilege clear.

Once everyone had gathered, we were led out the main gate to the far end of the practice fields where two large, jagged boulders jutted from the ground. Beyond lay a wide path that rose on a gentle hill and branched left and right around another bolder.

"The trail has most of the terrain you'll come across on patrol in the Gray," Lord Quill said. "It's mostly rocky, but there are some trees and plants that manage to grow here. The path is magically protected from the shadows, but you might still encounter wildlife. Most of the wildlife is harmless."

"So," Rider barked. "Get running. Once around the path. The sooner you finish, the longer rest you have before we assess your archery skills."

We all hurried to the entrance, with me and a couple of the fae at the front only because we'd been closest to the entrance.

"Take the righthand path," Talon called out just before we reached the split.

We went right and crested the hill. The path sloped down sharply and curved around the edge of a rocky outcropping then headed into a forest of twisted, black, scraggly trees that looked half dead.

But ahead, from the vantage of being on top of the hill, I could see more rocky, scraggly, jagged, gray land with mist curling around rocks and tree trunks, and beyond, wreathed in mist, stood the enormous, towering Shadow Gate.

It was closer than I'd expected, although the whole point of the Black Tower was to guard the Gate in the event it opened again. The overcast sky seemed to crowd down, and I knew exactly why this place was called the Gray. Everything was gray and damp and drab, and I had a feeling it was always like this or worse.

A shiver slid down my spine at the blatant reminder of where I was.

One of the fae behind me bumped my shoulder, jostling me out of his way as he ran down the hill, and I realized that I'd stopped to stare at the Gray when I should have been running.

I tore my attention away from the Shadow Gate, took a few jogged stepped along the path but another fae bumped me, then another.

"We know what you did," one of them hissed at me as he ran past.

"Mucking out the stables isn't punishment enough for endangering a brother," another said, hitting me hard and sending me stumbling.

"Thought you were too *noble* for the Guard and didn't bother with the rules?" Mikel sneered, shouldering me out of his way.

My toe caught on the uneven ground and I lost my balance. My shin hit a sharp rock jutting out of the ground at the edge of the path and I tumbled forward, the impact sending agony shooting through my bruised chest as I slid face-first the rest of the way down the path.

"Oh, sorry, *my lord*," Durand snickered, and he and Ambrose ran past chuckling.

The rest of the fae and all of the other humans ran past me as well shooting me disgusted or angry looks as I shoved up to my knees, my body throbbing from Edred's beating and a whole morning of shoveling and scrubbing.

The younger of the two heavy-set guys shot me an apologetic look but didn't stop to help me, and so did a couple of the farmers, and it was clear I was on my own. I'd endangered guardsmen last night by using the ring after dark and they didn't feel my current punishment was enough. The question was, would they stop at just knocking me down a rocky hill or was I going to need to sleep with my dagger under my pillow tonight?

CHAPTER 33
Sage

THE FALL RIPPED a hole in my pantleg, cut my shin — with a thankfully shallow cut — and scraped both my palms and my chin. The last of the novices ran around the outcropping and into the trees without stopping to help which stung more than the scrape on my chin.

I knew it shouldn't have. I was a nobleman and if most nobles were like Edred then it made perfect sense for everyone else to want to put me in my place. This was their only chance because we were now equals.

But even with the dirty looks I'd gotten in the great hall at the morning and midday meal, I hadn't expected the fae to start it. I'd expected them to be cold and distant, not wanting to bother themselves with a lowly human, and I didn't know if their involvement meant my sin of accidentally endangering their *brothers* was more serious than I first thought or if they were just being petty.

Whatever the reason, it meant my plan to go unnoticed had failed before I'd even started.

I pushed myself to my feet and ran after them. I wasn't the fastest runner and didn't have the stamina of the fae or those men who'd already been training to be warriors, but I managed to catch up to a few of the others and push past them.

The course twisted around the scraggly tree trunks and past more jagged outcroppings. Then the trees thinned, and the path followed the top of a narrow ridge with a sharp drop on either side. One wrong step and someone would end up tumbling down a steep slope of sharp shale into more scraggly, half-dead bushes on one side or a fast-moving river on the other.

I glanced behind me to confirm the men I'd passed weren't close enough to push me off then hurried forward before they were.

The scrubby side of the ridge rose, and the path plunged back into the trees, but the side with the river remained steep and dangerous to my right and I kept to the left, thankful that the men I'd passed were falling farther and farther behind.

Except I didn't know how long that would last. My body was starting to burn with the effort to keep running and I had no idea how much farther I had to go.

Ahead, the path made another sharp turn, and I ran out of the trees into a clearing as one of the novices ahead of me tried to run across a log bridge spanning a stream and fell the good five feet into the water below. A few other novices — none of them fae or the five trained humans — were wading through the hip-deep water or climbing the almost sheer bank on the other side to get out.

Which meant I was going to have to run across the log and hope I didn't fall, or jump down and then figure out how to climb up without help, since I doubted anyone was going to give me a hand up. Maybe if I got lucky I'd find a foothold—

One of the men braced his toe in a crack in the rocks but couldn't get a good enough foothold to lift himself up.

"Hey, give me a hand," he called up to a taller guy who'd managed to climb out by himself.

The man reached down and offered him a hand then glanced up and gave me a dark look.

"Me, too," said the man who'd fallen in the water when I'd rounded the curve as he waded toward them.

"Sure, but not *the lord*," the taller guy replied, as if his look hadn't been clear enough.

Swell. If I jumped down, I could get stuck in the ravine until someone came to help me or I'd have to risk going up or down the stream to find an easier way out. What were the odds that the easier way out was still within the path's magical protection?

All right. The log bridge then. It was narrow. I could probably straddle it and inch my way along. I'd be ridiculed if the guys on the other side saw what I was doing, but it was the best option since it was going to be impossible to climb the bank on the other side without help.

Straddling meant I wouldn't fall, but it would also leave me vulnerable... which meant I was going to have to wait for the men on the other side to run out of sight before attempting to cross.

Except I could hear the footsteps of the men behind me drawing closer and if they jumped into the stream while I was straddling the log, they could pull me down and I'd be back to the problem on being too short to get out.

Running and praying I didn't fall was my only option... and then praying I could dodge the guys on the other side before they shoved me off the ledge and into the stream.

I sucked in a deep breath and waited for the tall guy to reach to help the second guy up the bank, then ran as fast as I could. I just needed to keep my balance for a few steps, that was all.

My foot hit the center of the log then my other foot hit center, two more steps then I started to tilt to the side. My next step was on the log's edge. I had at least three more steps to go to get across but knew only one more was going to land on the log. *Crap crap crap crap.*

With a yell, I took that final step and dove for the other side. I flew over the rest of the log and curled into a ball at the last second. My shoulder and back hit the ground, the impact making the bruise on my chest complain, and I rolled up to my feet and kept going, bolting down the path before the men could grab me and toss me into the stream.

I ran, my lungs burning and my body throbbing, determined to put as much distance between us. They'd already passed me once and I hoped they'd only gotten ahead of me because I'd fallen down that first hill and not because they were actually faster than me.

But I didn't want to bet on that. I forced myself to keep moving forward, one foot in front of the other, until I fought my way up another steep slope and looked down on the two boulders marking the path's entrance and the practice field beyond. Lord Rider, Lord Quill, and Talon waited by the boulders while all the fae and just over a dozen humans sat or stood nearby in various stages of trying to regain their breaths.

Talon raised an eyebrow when I jogged off the path and Lord Rider narrowed his eyes.

"You've had your pants less than half a shift and you've already ripped them," he said his voice gruff.

"Better be more careful. You won't get new ones until the end of the second rotation."

"Yes, my lord," I murmured, dropping my gaze on instinct before remembering I was supposed to look up. Always look up.

I snapped my gaze back up but the damage had been done. Now everyone had seen how I demurred to the Lord Commander, and I could see in their appraising expressions and hard looks the knowledge that I was weak and they were going to take advantage of it. I'd seen that look in Edred's and Pylos's eyes, although their look had been darker, not just determined to show me I didn't belong or where my place actually was, but to take pleasure in hurting and belittling me.

"You all right?" Talon asked, his voice so low I almost didn't hear him, and it still sent a shiver of need rushing down my spine.

I didn't know how it was possible. He'd barely spoken, but just that whisper reminded my body of what I'd seen and felt and desired last night.

"Just tripped," I replied, and I found a mostly flat patch of rocky ground away from the others to catch my breath while we waited for the rest of the novices.

"Stupid *and* clumsy," someone said just loud enough for me to hear, making the group of men, both human and fae, snicker.

"Do you think he'll even bother to fix them?" someone else asked.

"Probably doesn't know how," another man replied.

The novices I'd passed at the log bridge crested the hill and staggered into the practice area, and a short while later the last group half jogged half walked over the hill, gasping, their chests heaving with the exertion.

"Follow me," Lord Rider commanded before the last group had even passed between the boulders.

He led us along the edge of the practice yard, keeping out of the way of the men sparring with and without weapons, to the archery targets. There were eight targets set up and the last eight people to finish the course were each given a bow and arrow and told to shoot first.

It seemed cruel that the men still out of breath weren't given a chance to calm their pulse. If the Lord Commander really wanted to see how well these men performed, he should have gone with the most rested first. Then he'd get an accurate assessment of everyone's skills.

The first group released their arrows. Six of the ten missed completely, while the other four hit the hay behind the target or the outside edge of the target.

"Next," Lord Rider barked, and Lord Quill called out the names of the next eight, including mine.

I took a bow from the heavy-set apprentice chef

and an arrow from Quill — glimpsing into his eyes for a second before managing to heave my attention away — and stepped up to the line in front of a target. The bow was my best weapon even though I preferred the sword, probably because size and strength didn't matter as much with a bow.

I drew in a slow breath and concentrated on calming my body like the armsmaster before Pylos had taught me. Be still, be calm, center myself in my body, and focus. Except everyone was watching me, waiting for me to fail, and while I'd had a bit of time to rest, my pulse was still a little fast from running.

The man beside me released his arrow, the *twang* of the bowstring biting into my concentration.

I sucked in another breath and released it. There wasn't anything else around, just the target in front of me, the bow and arrow in my hands, and the soft hint of a breeze coming from my right and slightly behind. The *twang* of more arrows being released grew farther and farther away and my attention narrowed to the small black circle in the center of the target and the whisper of wind.

Another breath in then release, and I nocked the arrow, raised the bow, and drew back the string. My muscles complained, my arms sore from mucking the stables and my chest throbbing from the bruise and falling down on the trail, and my palms and chin stung where I'd scraped them.

I shoved those sensations aside, drew in one final breath, aimed — taking into account the distance and the breeze — and released the arrow. It shot true, landing in the center of the black dot with a solid *thud*. *Perfect shot!*

A murmur swept through the men behind me. See, I wasn't completely useless. I bit back a satisfied smile, since gloating was rude and I didn't want to give them more reason to hate me, and turned to hand my bow to the next novice. The other novices looked at me, some clearly shocked that I'd actually hit the target, while Lord Quill's expression turned appraising, and Talon smiled, clearly pleased at my success.

Pride warmed my chest. This was the first time anyone other than my first armsmaster had looked at me with approval for doing the thing I loved that as a woman I wasn't supposed to do. I'd hit the mark and no one was going to yell at me for not behaving properly.

I slid my attention to Lord Rider. He didn't look impressed like everyone else. "That's only a good shot if you hadn't taken forever to make it. A shadow isn't going to let you stand around and wait for you to get ready. You'd have been dead twice over before you'd even raised your bow," he said then looked away from me, his dismissal clear. "Next."

The warmth in my chest chilled as the next group took their positions. This had three of the two experienced humans and a few fae and while they got close to the black mark in the center none of them hit it. Except that didn't make me feel better. They all just raised their bows and fired without taking any time to center themselves and focus, making Lord Rider look at them with gruff satisfaction.

And I couldn't figure out why that stung. I wasn't supposed to be impressing Lord Rider or anyone else. I was just supposed to keep my head down until Sawyer was safe. But I'd made a perfect shot and he hadn't even acknowledged it as good. Of course, he was right. Even if I'd had a bow last night, I wouldn't have had a chance of using it before those shadow monsters had come after me.

But knowing that still didn't make it hurt less. I hadn't done anything right since I'd come here, and while I should have been used to not being acknowledged and browbeaten, a small part of me had hoped it would be different. Here I wasn't a woman. I was supposed to have value. But my fellow novices and probably most of the Guard thought I was an arrogant noble.

CHAPTER 34

Sage

THE ARCHERY TEST finished with three of the fae, Mikel, and Ambrose hitting the mark in the center in a fraction of the time I'd taken, then we were all ushered away from the archery range to a flat area that had a large circle carved into the rocky ground. Beside the circle someone had laid out a variety of practice weapons from short swords, long daggers, large two-handed swords, and even a couple of battleaxes.

Lord Quill called the name of one of the humans who'd done poorly on the archery test. He'd also been in the group that had finished the running trail after me but hadn't been the man who'd arrived last. He was told to select a practice weapon and step into the ring.

Lord Rider stepped in to fight him and the man, a skinny man whose breathing had sounded a little like Sawyer's when he'd staggered off the running trail, froze. His eyes widened and his blade, a thin longsword that was actually a good fit for his size and strength, started to tremble.

"No head, no hands, first one to three touches," Lord Quill said.

"Begin," Talon called out, and the skinny novice jumped as if he'd been bitten.

Lord Rider slowly moved to the right, studying his opponent, but it was clear the novice had no combat training at all. He didn't move with Lord Rider to keep his weapon between them, only followed the large fae with his eyes, and his stance was all wrong, his feet too close together. A moderately strong push and he'd lose his balance.

Lord Rider stepped in and did a slow, tentative tap to the man's shoulder, surprising me. I would have thought he'd have done a full aggressive attack on everyone. He could easily overpower most of the novices here, certainly all of the humans, but then that wouldn't give him a good assessment of this novice's skills. And if I really thought about it, he'd been kind and gentle with me in the garden, which made me wonder if his gruff, angry demeanor was an act or not.

The skinny novice jerked away from Lord Rider's attack, not even trying to get his blade up to block, tripped, and landed on his butt, making a few of the fae and the experienced humans chuckle.

"I've seen enough," Lord Rider said as he stepped away from his opponent. "Next."

The next few novices, all humans, varied between weak and highly skilled, and after the first few, I realized, Lord Quill was mixing up the skill levels, so Lord Rider wasn't fighting too many highly skilled fighters in a row.

With the humans who clearly had no experience, Lord Rider always started with the tentative swing to the shoulder — switching it up between left and right. For those who demonstrated more experience in how they stood, held their weapons, and moved those initial few steps, his attacks were faster and more varied.

I watched how he moved, trying to determine any weakness, but as expected, he was never off balance and his guard was always there to block. He'd even been able to block when Durand jabbed in then twisted his wrist and slid the tip of his blade over Lord Rider's toward his chest in a move that wasn't easy to do with a heavy longsword. The move had made Lord Rider's eyes widen with a hint of surprise and then crinkle at the corners with pleasure for a second before his stoic, gruff expression returned.

Then Lord Quill called the first fae novice. The man was just as big and bulky as Lord Rider and moved with the same dangerous grace.

They slowly circled in an attempt to gage each

other's skill level then the novice lunged in, the movement fast and fluid. Lord Rider blocked, and they exchanged a flurry of powerful blows and blocks, demonstrating just how much Lord Rider had been holding back with the humans, even Durand.

I'd never seen anything like it. They were both so powerful and fast. None of the men at Herstind had been able to fight like that, not even Pylos or Edred, and for a moment I couldn't understand why the fae bothered to work with us humans at all. But then if they didn't, defending the Gray would fall entirely on them and, because the Black Guard was half human half fae, it was clear they didn't want that.

Still, how many fae guardsmen looked down on us weaker humans? I hadn't noticed that kind of divide during the morning or midday meal, but then I'd only really noticed the looks everyone had been giving me.

But then Mikel's name was called, and he gave a showing almost as good as the fae novice with powerful strikes and quick movements. He even managed to get two points on Lord Rider before the Lord Commander had gotten his three points and won the fight.

The assessment went on like that, good then bad, moderately skilled then fae.

One of the younger, inexperienced novices mumbled about all the fae being so good and another replied, "They chose serving the Black Guard, so they know they're going to need to know how to fight and prepare for it."

"They volunteer?" another novice asked.

"We humans should do that as well," Mikel said as the novice in the ring tripped over his own feet and fell. "It's stupid to just send anyone."

"Embarrassing too," Durand added. "The fae must think we're useless sending men who don't know how to hold a sword and runts who are stupid."

"Next," Lord Rider growled as the novice he'd just defeated picked himself and his sword off the ground and hurried out of the ring.

"Ambrose," Lord Quill called out and Ambrose hopped up from his seat on the ground, grabbed a practice sword and stepped into the ring.

Like all the other fights, Lord Rider started circling him, judging his hold on his weapon and his movement before lunging in with an attack.

Ambrose parried and countered, and it was clear that just like Mikel and Durand that Ambrose hadn't lied about his past experience. He wasn't on the same level as the fae or Mikel, but he was still good. He wouldn't have been pinned to the ground by a shadow monster. His first swings would have struck true not just cut off spikes. Of course, he wouldn't have been stupid enough to use the fae ring after dark.

He got a point on Lord Rider before their fight was done and stepped out of the ring with a smug grin that

Mikel, Duran, and the other experienced humans returned.

Then my name was called, and Lord Rider slid his dark, verging-on-angry glare at me.

My heart leaped into my throat, and I headed to the collection of practice weapons and took the time to choose the lightest of the shorter swords, making the others whisper and laugh at the attention I was paying to the weapons. But my arms and chest still hurt, and they were only going to get worse, which meant if I didn't want to embarrass myself by not being able to hold up my weapon for the entire fight, I needed the lightest weapon possible.

Lord Rider's eyes narrowed as I stepped into the ring and took a fighting stance, his expression reminding me of the look Edred had given me when I'd blocked his strike at Sawyer, making my pulse pound harder.

The Lord Commander had held back with the other humans, but would he hold back with me? Did he feel the same way the others did about my mistake last night and was he going to take this opportunity to give me a lesson like Edred used to?

If I was smart, I'd take the beating and let him vent his frustration like I'd done with Edred. Except with Edred, I hadn't been able to fight back. I'd had to pretend I didn't know how to fight to avoid a worse punishment.

But here, I could actually fight. I didn't have a hope of winning, but maybe I could get in a touch before Lord Rider beat me down.

The thought sent a thrill of excitement rushing through me. I could fight. I could actually fight and not worry about the repercussions. I could test my skill, learn more, learn enough that if I survived this mess and didn't end up in prison for the rest of my life, I might actually be able to become a legendary swordmaiden.

Lord Rider started circling and I followed, keeping my weapon between us and my stance balanced, my body thrumming with sudden exhilaration.

One good touch. That was my goal.

Except from the look in his eyes, I doubted Lord Rider was going to treat me like the other inexperienced novices so I couldn't expect a tentative swing at my shoulder — which would have been the ideal moment to get my touch since he wouldn't know how fast or skilled I was and I'd be able to catch him off guard. That meant I was going to have to look for another opening and the sooner the better since as soon as Lord Rider got into the fight, I'd be beaten down and that would be the end of it.

His front foot shifted, announcing his swing a fraction of a second before his sword swept out to my right shoulder. The swing was painfully slow, shocking me, and added to that rush of excitement. I didn't know why he'd decided I didn't know how to fight at all when I'd said I had some experience, but it meant I actually had a chance of scoring a point. I had to seize the opportunity. If he was going to give me the opening, I'd take it.

I ducked under his blade and sliced at his chest in one quick fluid motion like the previous armsmaster had taught me. But Lord Rider snapped his blade down, blocking my strike, and I realized it was a trap to lull me into a sense of false confidence.

The hard impact of our blades connecting threatened my grip, and I twisted out of the way of his counter jab, knowing if I made contact with his blade again so soon, I'd lose my grip on my weapon. But Lord Rider didn't give me time to catch my breath and regroup like he had with the other humans. He pressed his attack, forcing me to scramble back to get out of the way of his flurry of strokes.

"Almost at the edge," Talon called out, and even though it hadn't been said, I knew I'd lose the fight if I left the ring.

Lord Rider swung at my shoulder with a force that would probably break bone if it made contact and certainly tear my blade from my grip if I blocked. I dove under the strike, rolling back toward the center of the ring then twisted back to him and lunged. It was a reckless move but if I didn't at least try to fight back he'd have me running around the ring until I was out of breath. And damn it! I was going to score my point.

He blocked my lunge, countered with another hard swing to my shoulder and I bolted behind him, somehow managing — by a miracle no doubt — to slide the tip of my blade against his hip before he jerked out of the way and almost batted my blade out of my hands.

"Touch, Sawyer," Talon called out as I rushed out of Lord Rider's reach and turned back to face him.

My chest and arms and hell, my whole body, throbbed with the exertion of the last two days and I fought to get my breathing under control, while Lord Rider, even after having fought all but a few of the novices already, didn't even look winded.

Behind him, the other novices stared at me, shocked, and I realized that I, the runt — a girl — had actually managed to score a touch on the Lord Commander of the Black Guard.

The thought sent a swell of pride and rush of excitement surging through me until I realized scoring a point on Lord Rider didn't make sense because he was so much better and faster and stronger than me.

He'd let me get the touch in, which confused me even more and that joy turned sour. I wanted to earn that touch fair and square. I didn't want him taking pity on me because I was small. Except if he was taking pity on me, why was he coming after me like he wanted to punish me?

Lord Rider snarled and came at me again with another flurry of strikes. I leaped back, trying to keep the distance between us, but he moved faster, stepped into range and gave me no time to duck or dive out of the way. His heavy sword swept down toward my head even though that was an illegal strike, and I heaved my blade up to block the strike, squeezing the grip in both hands to hold onto my weapon.

But the impact twisted me to the side and tore the sword from my hands, sending the weapon clattering over the rocky ground.

Lord Rider lunged and snapped the edge of his practice weapon against my side. The hit was firm, but not hard. He'd pulled his stroke at the last second, but the edge hit my massive, still-fresh bruise from yesterday's beating and shot agony through my chest.

I clenched my jaw against my scream of pain but couldn't stop myself from falling to my knees and clutching my side. Tears pricked my eyes and I fought to hold them back. I was *not* going to give them the satisfaction of seeing me cry, no matter how much that had hurt.

"Jeez, can't even take a hit," Mikel sneered.

"Next," Lord Rider barked, making my cheeks heat in shame. He wasn't even going to bother fighting me to three touches. One touch and I was out like the novices who didn't know how to fight.

But I did know how to fight and I wanted to keep going. Needed to. I needed to score my point fair and square. It didn't matter that my body throbbed in agony and that I didn't stand a chance against Lord Rider. I was going to score a damned touch.

Except that wasn't the point of why I was here.

Why did I have to keep reminding myself of that?

Bide my time until Sawyer was safe. They were going to find out eventually I was a girl. Being obstinate and demanding Lord Rider wear me down and beat me up wasn't the way to blend in with the other novices.

"Come on, move it," Rider growled at me, making me flinch with the memory of Edred's beatings. "I want this done before the seventh bell rings."

"Yes—" I bit the inside of my cheek, stopping *my lord* from coming out, grabbed my practice weapon, and scrambled out of the ring.

CHAPTER 35
Talon

SAWYER CLUTCHED his side and scurried out of the fighting ring, his eyes downcast making me want to punch Rider. The boy had put up an incredible fight and should have gotten more than a "move it."

He'd actually scored a point on Rider something none of us expected and while Rider had been holding back, it hadn't been by as much as I would have expected for someone so young and small. The boy had known before stepping into the ring his best chance at getting a point was at the beginning of the fight before Rider had fully assessed his abilities, and if Rider hadn't been as quick and skilled as he was, Sawyer would have gotten that first point right at the start.

As it was, the boy knew he wasn't strong enough to

face Rider head on and had used his speed to dodge Rider's attacks until he saw an opening.

His skill was a pleasant surprise and something we could definitely build on. Out of all the novices, he probably had the most potential because he was so young and hadn't had nearly the same amount of training as the three men trained from birth to become guardsmen or the soldiers. Perhaps killing that hound hadn't been dumb luck like Rider had said.

That said, Rider's strike hadn't been that hard. He'd pulled it at the last second like he always did when he was sparring. It shouldn't have brought the boy to his knees with his face twisted in agony. But I didn't think it was because he was a weak nobleman who couldn't take a hit. The way he flinched from Rider's sharp command to leave the circle suggested he was well used to taking hits, which meant he was foolishly trying to hide an injury.

Rider scored a point, tapping the thigh of the next novice — an inexperienced farmer — and shouldered the man making him lose his balance and fall over.

"Next," he growled, his expression hard and angry. His gaze leaped to Sawyer — who was looking at the ground, not making eye contact with anyone — then back to the group of novices as Quill called out the final novice's name.

It was clear Rider was pissed at himself for hurting the boy... and pissed at the boy for hiding his injury. If he'd known Sawyer was hurt, he might not have made the boy spend all morning in the stables and he certainly would have been more careful about where and how he scored his point.

That and hiding an injury wasn't a good way to start a career in the Guard. Just like going through the ring after dark, keeping an injury a secret meant you weren't at your best and that could get a fellow guardsman killed.

The next novice was a fae with average skill that was obvious in how he reacted to Rider's first attack, but Rider didn't pull back. He went at the fae full force as if he needed an outlet for his frustration with Sawyer and scored three quick points leaving a stunned fae standing in the circle probably wondering what the hell had just happened.

"The rest of this rotation you'll have chores in the morning and more assessment in the afternoon, then the real training begins," Rider said, his voice gruff. "In a few rotations I'll be starting the competition for elite positions and if you can prove to me that you can hold your own like any other guardsman, I'll let you, a novice, try for a spot."

That perked up all the humans who knew how to fight except Sawyer.

"How many fae spots are there?" one of the fae asked. A few of them looked hopeful that they'd be able to qualify for an elite position so soon, but the rest were skeptical and rightly so since we usually needed to replace more humans than fae.

"Seven. Five hunters and two for the Gold Tower," Rider replied. "Which means there's a spot for two humans in the Gold Tower, two in the White Tower, and seven in hunting teams."

"That's eleven spots," one of the experience humans whispered to another.

"And you're competing against the other experienced guardsmen who want a place," I added, which was a good number of men, although not everyone. Some of the men, both human and fae, were content with their regular duties. There were fewer privileges but there was also less responsibility and less danger.

"But until then you're on the novices' rotation," Quill said, bringing us back on topic like he always did. "Don't forget to check your assignment outside the quartermaster's rooms and be ready to work at the second bell."

The seventh bell rang.

"Everyone pick up a practice weapon and take it to the indoor practice hall then you're dismissed for the evening," Rider said.

He shot me a look, one that I knew after years of working together meant, "find out how badly the boy is injured," then he picked up a battle axe and led the way back to the castle.

The men each grabbed a weapon and followed him

and Quill back to the castle. Sawyer hung back, and from the whispered comments from the other novices, I didn't blame him. The humans had decided he didn't fit in while it looked like the fae thought mucking out the stables wasn't punishment enough for foolishly using the ring after dark. And as much as I wanted to tell everyone to stop being assholes, it was better if it came from Sawyer.

That said, I was going to make sure Ash kept an eye on the boy. There'd been a spark in his eyes when he'd stepped into the ring to fight Rider and I doubted a few mean words, even if they came from Rider, were enough to extinguish it, but we'd had human novices commit suicide before for less.

The apprentice chef — who really didn't belong in the guard but would be a good addition to the two main cooks in charge of the kitchens — shot Sawyer a quick, sad look.

"I can't believe you scored a point," he said, grabbing a pair of long daggers and hurrying after the rest of the group before Sawyer could answer.

"I didn't score a point," Sawyer said to himself.

"Pretty sure I saw a point and called it." I grabbed the three remaining practice swords and held out the lightest one, hilt first, for Sawyer to take.

"The Lord Commander gave it to me." Sawyer's gaze slipped up to mine then jerked away and he took the offered sword. He still held his side like it hurt but just like when he'd first stumbled into my bathing room and I'd climbed out naked and exposed him being fae-touched, I got the impression that one wrong move would scare him away.

"Rider picks one skill level above the one he thinks you're at," I said, heading after the others, my pace slow hoping Sawyer would walk with me. "Just enough to see how far you can stretch then slowly builds depending on how you respond. That point was all yours and it shocked the hell out of him. Everyone, actually."

"But that doesn't make the point mine. I'd never had scored if it had been a real fight, and he ended it after he scored his like with the other inexperienced novices." He ran a hand through his red hair, mussing the already wild locks. "I don't know why it bothers me. There's no way I'd win a fight against him." He snorted. "Unless I was fifty yards away with a bow." Then his expression turned sour. "And he gave me the time to line up my shot."

"The point was yours. With the exception of most of the fae novices, Mikel, Ambrose, and Durand, you'd have scored a point on any of the other novices. That includes Bramwell and Hamelin." One of whom had been raised to be a guardsman and the other had been a professional soldier before his name had been drawn in the lottery.

"Bramwell and Hamelin are slow, but one hit from them and I'd be seeing stars for days," Sawyer said.

"And that one hit from Rider could have seriously hurt you," I replied, trying to broach the topic of his injury without making him clam up or run away. "He pulled it, but if you have broken ribs, he could have done more damage."

Thankfully, from the way he'd stopped holding his side and was breathing normally, it didn't look like the injury was that bad... although I was getting the impression Sawyer was too stubborn for his own good. If Rider hadn't ended the fight, he would have kept going, and I suspected from the looks a bunch of the novices had shot each other when I'd asked Sawyer about it, his trip on the running trail wasn't because he was clumsy, either.

I grabbed Sawyer's arm and stopped him before we passed through the pasture gate. "If you're injured, you report to the infirmary."

Sawyer froze, his gaze locked on mine, and his lips parted on a sharp, soft breath. Then red, brighter than his hair, raced over his pale cheeks and down his neck, disappearing beneath the collar of his too-big shirt and jerkin.

"It's just a bruise," he breathed.

"You should go to the infirmary and have Flint check you out," I pressed.

"It's fine. It's just fresh." His voice trembled along

with his body and panic filled his eyes as he tried to look away from me and couldn't.

I hadn't expected his reaction to my unwanted allure to be so powerful. I wasn't even naked. But he was so ensnared, I could see his pulse fluttering in the large vein in his neck. And while I should have let him go and broken eye contact, I knew if I did, he'd continue to lie about his injury.

"Prove it," I forced out, my insides twisting with shame. "Show me."

CHAPTER 36
Talon

SAWYER'S EYES flashed wide at my command and the panic grew. "You want me to what?"

"Take off your shirt and show me." Goddess above I was disgusting. I hated using my allure like this. I hated using my allure at all and yet in this case, I needed to be able to tell Rider that the boy was all right and he hadn't done more damage by sparring with him, or I needed to drag the boy to Flint and get him fixed up or put on bedrest.

Boy was Rider going to be pissed at himself if he forced someone who should have been on bedrest to muck out the stables all morning. Of course, if that was the case, part of it was Sawyer's fault for not saying anything.

"I, ah…"

The fear in his eyes grew and his breath turned sharp as he tried to look away from me but couldn't, reminding me that he was just a boy and human. What he felt for me came with other issues, ones that might have been the reason he'd flinched at Rider's sharp dismissal and how I knew he had experience with being beaten.

Fuck. What was wrong with me?

I released him and forced myself through the pasture gate into the bailey. A few of the novices were on the other side of the bailey headed toward the barracks and Quill stood in the doorway of the indoor practice hall, waiting for me and the last of the weapons.

"Quill," I said, grabbing Quill and pulling him back inside the building. As feared, even though I'd stopped making eye contact, my allure on Sawyer was still strong and it compelled him to stumble after us. "Show Quill."

"I'm not— It's just a bruise. I swear," Sawyer insisted, his voice regaining strength now that he wasn't captured within my gaze. "There's no point in bothering the healer. I— I'm used to it." He undid the clasps of his jerkin with trembling fingers and raised his shirt just enough to reveal the large dark purple bruise staining across his ribs and up his chest. "The Marquis of Herstind March has a temper."

Quill stiffened, his sudden change in demeanor

shocking and not like Quill at all. "What about your sister? Does he hurt your sister?"

Sawyer's hands shook harder as he tried to reclasp his jerkin.

"I'm going back," Quill said, taking Sawyer's silence as a yes. "Tell Rider we'll discuss the novices in the Garden."

What the hell? Where had this come from? There were only a few hours of daylight left in the Gray. If Quill left now, he wouldn't be able to return until morning.

He shoved past me to get to the door, but Sawyer caught his arm, stopping him.

"Don't. She's not there. I—" More panic flashed through Sawyer's expression. "It's why I used the ring so late yesterday. I couldn't leave her at the castle."

"So, she safe?" Quill asked, his reaction shocking me.

I had no idea why Quill was so interested in Sawyer's sister. I'd never seen him interested in a human woman before. He didn't even visit the brothel in Lehyrst with the other Guardsmen. And while yes, it went against everything we believed in to hurt a woman, there were a lot of human women being hurt in the human's realm and we had to turn a blind eye to it. What made Sawyer's sister so special?

"She's safe." Sawyer's gaze dropped to his feet, adding to my frustration.

He was so timid. I knew he had a spark within him.

I'd seen a glimmer of it when he fought Rider and he'd killed a hound for goodness' sake, but I suspected his submission had been beaten into him and was going to be a hard habit to break.

Then, much to my surprise, he jerked his attention back up as if he'd suddenly remembered what I'd told him last night. "She's safe and I'm fine. I still have half a shift of stable duty at the eighth bell and I'm hungry. Am I dismissed?"

From the set of his jaw, it was clear I'd have to push to get anything more from him and I didn't want to push him. His spark had returned, but that didn't mean it was here to stay.

That, and I needed to know what the hell was wrong with Quill, and I couldn't demand answers in front of Sawyer. Quill was acting like a soul-bonded male with his sudden need to rescue Sawyer's sister, which was impossible because she was human and they'd barely met.

"Yes. Go." I took the practice sword from him and waved him off, watching him run out the door then turned to Quill. "What the hell was that?"

"Nothing." Quill said, heading for the door as well.

I blocked his path and met his gaze, trying to figure out what was going on with him. "That wasn't nothing. You were ready to leave the Gray without a second thought. You only met Sawyer's sister briefly and she's not fae so there's no bond."

"I know." The look in his emerald eyes slid from frightened to grief stricken and confused. "I know," he repeated as if he couldn't make himself believe it, then his shoulders sagged and he stepped close, pressing his forehead against mine, his breath feathering over my cheeks and lips. "She's human. Her life is so short. She doesn't even know me. And I can't stop thinking about her. I've been trying all day and I can't. Every time I look at the boy, I think of her... can *see* her in him. Which is crazy. I barely got a look at either of them, but I know they're siblings and I—"

I dropped the practice weapons and wrapped my arms around him, holding him close.

"It's a fascination. Not a bond," I murmured against his jaw, more to convince myself than him. We both knew fae couldn't bond with humans so what he felt wasn't more than a sudden, shocking obsession, not a soul bond.

"I know it is, and yet—" His breath picked up. "I can't seem to convince myself of that no matter how impossible it is."

My throat tightened. It sure sounded like he'd fallen for her, and while it was rare, some fae men did fall instantly in love with their mates before the female even acknowledge them. Except that was only for bonded mates and bonding was only ever between fae.

So, what he felt was impossible. But he wanted a female mate so badly and knew in his soul that having one was impossible because he had no magic. He'd latched onto this human female in a desperate, probably unconscious need to fulfill his heart's desire.

"She'll break your heart," I whispered.

And that would break mine. I loved Quill so deeply it hurt. It had taken me far too long to figure out how I felt about Quill and by then I'd spent years succumbing to the desire of the shadow trapped within me. Just like it compelled humans to desire me, it compelled me to desire them— hell, to desire everyone. Human, fae, man, woman, it didn't matter.

I'd slept with almost everyone who was interested because I had to and had convinced Quill and myself that what we had was casual. Just like the relationship a lot of fae men had with each other.

And then I'd realized the truth. That I was desperately in love with Quill *and* that the shadow took something it needed from my sexual partners. I weakened them when we had sex, but I couldn't ignore the compulsion to have sex, or I'd lose control of the monster inside me. And that could never be allowed to happen again.

But I knew Quill wouldn't take bonding vows with me because he wanted a family and wasn't ready to let go of that dream even though we both knew it was never going to happen.

Except falling for a human wouldn't give him a family, either.

"Guess it's only fair she breaks my heart," he said, sliding his cheek against mine and burying his face in my shoulder, "because I think I broke hers by delivering her brother's summons to the Gray."

I clung to him, fighting the urge to turn the embrace into something more. He needed comfort. He didn't need sex. Besides, we'd had sex last night in the Garden and I didn't want to weaken him further.

"He said she's safe," I murmured into his hair.

My thoughts leaped to the ugly bruise marring Sawyer's torso. I shouldn't have just taken his word for it that he wasn't hurt worse. A bruise that size and that dark indicated a serious beating. He might not have broken ribs, but they could be cracked. Still— "He's better off here. He'll get roughed up in practice and on duty, but he won't be beaten just because." And he certainly won't be beaten because he was fae-touched. "Here he has a fighting chance. And by bringing him here, she got away, too."

Quill sucked in a sharp breath and shoved whatever he was feeling back behind the mask he'd built up over the years that made him a good captain. No matter what he was feeling, he always gave a sense of control. He was the calm to Rider's ferocious determination and my charming allure... while Ash was the shadow watching our backs.

And if I was smart, I'd ask Ash to watch Sawyer's back. If the other novices didn't back down, the boy could reach a point where he'd be forced to fight back or break, and I really didn't want to see the boy break.

CHAPTER 37
Rider

I PICKED at my meal of venison and root vegetables knowing eating was a practical necessity for a warrior but unable to concentrate on the job. Stunned green eyes and brilliant red hair kept flitting through my mind's eye, and the more I thought about it, the more I was sure she'd been too stunned to know where she'd been last night.

I shouldn't have let Talon scare her off. I should have taken the moment to find someone I trusted to take care of her. I—

Why the hell couldn't I stop thinking of her? I'd been thinking of her since I'd left the Garden last night. I couldn't seem to get her out of my mind.

Sage.

Her name rolled around and around in my head. I didn't know her. Didn't care about her. Sure, she'd been new and vulnerable, but it hadn't been my business. I didn't want a mate. I'd had a mate, found that one woman who'd made my soul sing, and now she was dead. I didn't want to replace her. I couldn't. And I sure as hell didn't want the Goddess to force a mate on me, either.

Talon scaring her away had been for the best.

Except I couldn't make myself believe that. What if Wells had found her again? He was one of a handful of young men determined to be mated who aggressively pursued all available women. And while many women loved that, others were intimidated by it, and given how Sage had run away from him instead of telling him off, I suspected she was a woman of the latter group. Winning her bond wouldn't come by pursuit. It came by letting her see your soul and understanding just how special it was when she let you see hers.

Like it had been with Isemay. She'd been ferocious when she needed to be, a match to my wolf's nature, but she'd also been careful with her heart and soul. The human men of her world had scarred her, made her wary of opening up, but when she had, it had been like one of those rare moments when the sun cut through the mist in the Gray.

Had Sage been hurt the same way? Maybe she was just shy. There were so few women they were precious and there were some sects that kept them safe and sheltered, preparing them at the last moment for what to expect in the Garden while training them to look for mates in the men among the sect. Perhaps Sage had grown up in a family in one of those sects and manifested sooner than expected.

"For the love of— eat the damn carrot," Talon said, snapping me out of my reverie.

"What?" I stared at him sitting across the table in my private suite, a cup of wine in his hand, his own meal finished.

He gave a pointed glare to the carrot piece I'd been pushing around my plate. "Just because you favor meat doesn't mean you don't also need vegetables."

"And did you hear the last two things I said?" Quill asked, using his bread to sop up the last of the gravy on his plate.

"You want to test Winter and Rue's magic," I repeated back then shoved the carrot into my mouth.

Quill sighed and ran his hands through his short, blond hair. "Not the last two things I said. I said of the humans there are nine who we can put into advanced training right away. Mikel, Durand, Hamelin, Bramwell, Ambrose, Aldis, Jokin, Sivis, and Sawyer."

There were a few other novices on the borderline who we might want to put in advanced training once this first rotation was done, but those nine were definitely the most skilled of the group... Sawyer being a shocking surprise.

I'd thought because he'd been stupid enough to

use the ring after dark and so damn small, he'd have minimal weapons training. Usually extensive training built muscle, something the boy didn't have much of. Of course, if he was only sixteen, he could still be waiting on a growth spurt. Goddess, I hope he was. I didn't think we'd ever had a guardsman of such slight stature before.

That said, the boy could fight, and he had a good eye at archery. Whoever had taught him, had taught him competition shooting, stilling himself and focusing solely on the target, but with a bit of practice he'd be able to speed that up. If, of course, the chaos of battle didn't send him running.

Except I already knew it wouldn't. He'd been losing the fight against the hounds when Grefin and I had saved him, but he'd still been fighting. That and before I figured out he was a hell of lot better with the sword than I — and probably anyone — had first assumed, he'd managed to dodge my attacks and even score a point until I'd raised my skill level to that of the top human novices.

At least until I'd scored my first hit and brought him to his knees.

I bit back a growl of frustration at the boy for not mentioning that he was hurt but mostly at myself for being so angry with him last night that I hadn't bothered to check him out after hauling him into the Tower's bailey. He'd looked shaken but he hadn't been bleeding and Grefin said he'd climbed the stairs to his room without problem. Hell, even Talon hadn't said anything after the boy had stumbled across him in the bathhouse.

And while Talon had assured me Sawyer didn't need a healer, it didn't make me feel better that his guardian had beaten him, and I was now punishing him for protecting his sister. He still shouldn't have come through the ring after dark and it still didn't sound like he'd known how dangerous that was, so he still needed to be reprimanded, but that didn't make me feel better.

Maybe I could suggest to Talon to tell Sawyer to appeal his punishment. He had a right to do so and probably didn't even know that, either.

But given how the boy had taken my punishment and the snide remarks from the other novices, I doubted he would. That and just taking a rotation of stable duty with an extra half shift after the evening meal would go a long way to easing the anger of the other guardsmen. Speaking up would just make him look more like a spoiled nobleman that the other novices thought he was, even if Kit, Payne, Lewin, and even Grefin had reported the boy was anything but.

He was reeling like all human novices were when they first arrived, more so because his arrival hadn't been pleasant. That was all. Just like a certain red-haired beauty had been reeling.

Fucking Shadows. I had to stop thinking about her. "We'll put those nine into the accelerated training with the fae novices when the initial first rotation is done," I forced out.

Talon sat forward. "Not Sawyer. He's a child and he's timid. A few extra rotations with the other novices will be good for him."

"The humans say he's a man and he already knows the basics," Quill replied. "He'll be bored and think it's another punishment. He has extraordinary potential. He could become an elite hunter. But if we're not smart, we'll break his spirit."

Which was the biggest challenge with the human novices. The fae chose to be in the Guard. They had to commit to fifty years of service, but most stayed for the rest of their lives unless they were soul bonded with a woman or chose a male mate and wanted to settle down.

The humans were here for life whether they wanted to be or not. Some saw it as their purpose before they were even summoned, but the rest had to discover that it was their purpose or find peace with it. Those who'd had a full life, like our new smith who'd had three children and a wife before his name had been drawn, struggled, and it was a delicate balance between pushing them to turn them into decent Guardsmen and not breaking their already damaged spirit.

"I'm not sure he *is* a man." Talon took a long sip from his cup then sighed. "We all saw the way he fought. He studied you with the other novices, knew his best chance at scoring a point was right at the beginning before you figured out how fast he is. Which means he's smart. He's also not arrogant and doesn't parade around like some of the other noblemen we've had to deal with, so Grefin's idea that he thought he was too important to pay attention doesn't make sense."

"Maybe the humans messed up and a priest didn't give him the talk," Quill said.

"Or maybe he's not sixteen yet," Talon replied.

That thought made me almost as angry as forcing a father to abandon his children. Except human children weren't rare like fae children and neither were female mates. Family wasn't as precious to the humans as it was to us, and it wasn't my place to try to fix how the humans selected their half of the Black Guard. Even if Sawyer wasn't sixteen, he was probably close enough.

"He's been bound to the Tower. He's a Guardsman now," I said, my voice gruffer than I intended.

If Talon was right, then the humans really were sending me children now. Thank the Goddess this child at least knew how to swing a sword and hadn't pissed himself squaring off against me or the hounds.

"We can keep him off the most dangerous shifts for

a while," I said. "But the rest of the men have sacrificed enough lieu time. They're getting tired and tired men start fights and have accidents. We need more bodies and he's a body."

"And what good will he be if he's killed?" Talon insisted, sitting forward and glaring at me as if that would get me to change my mind. Which he knew wouldn't. It never did. "I'd rather we risk breaking his confidence in himself than throwing him to the shadows."

"No. There's no point in even debating this," I growled, spearing another piece of carrot with more force than I intended. Talon was right. The boy shouldn't be thrown into active duty so quickly, but we couldn't afford to hold him back.

"There sure as hell is. He's a child. He doesn't even know himself." Talon's breath picked up and the shadow trapped under his skin that he couldn't get rid of but usually managed to keep under control by regularly having sex started swirling up his neck.

Quill set a hand on Talon's knee, making Talon tense.

"Fuck," he hissed as if he'd just realized he was losing control of his shadow. He ran his hands through his hair and drew in sharp breaths, trying to calm himself and his shadow.

"When was the last time you fucked?" I asked. I couldn't afford to have him lose control, not when I needed him to help me with the novices, especially the boy he'd gotten so worked up about.

"Last night," Quill replied, his expression tight with worry.

"Well, you need to fuck someone tonight as well," I growled back. "I don't want to have to put you in the infirmary because your shadow took over."

Talon snorted. "Are you making an offer?"

"If that's what you need," I growled back, making Quill's eyebrows rise in surprise, because while Talon and I had fucked before, I hadn't had sex with him or anyone since I'd mated Isemay. "You're losing your shit over a boy and with barely a day after sex. That's not like you at all."

"A boy who's fae-touched," Quill added softly, making Talon shoot him a dark look.

"That isn't your secret to share. I'm not sure he fully realized the truth until he walked in on me in the bath-house last night."

Ah. Well, that explained it. Talon's shadow wanted Sawyer, but Talon was the kind of man who didn't take advantage of someone. If the boy didn't know he was fae-touched, then Talon's magic was influencing him toward something he might not be ready for, and Talon wouldn't be able to tell if the boy was a willing participant or not.

"I'd rather you find someone else, but I'll feed your shadow if I have to," I said. "But it has to happen tonight, and we're putting Sawyer into the advanced training."

"Fine." The muscles in Talon's jaw tightened and a hint of shadow curled up his neck. "Let's get to the Garden and find out what Ash has learned. Then I'll find someone to fuck."

"And we need to warn him that we've got three novices who should be on suicide watch," Quill said.

My pulse picked up at the thought of going to the Garden. Would she be there? Would she still be just as stunned?

Fuck. What the hell was wrong with me? I had to stop thinking about her. Just. Stop.

CHAPTER 38

Sage

I ATE the evening meal with Kit, Payne, and Lewin painfully aware that even more men watched me with disgust and anger as well as now a hint of curiosity. Hushed conversations came to an abrupt halt when I drew near, and it was obvious they were talking about me. Everyone in the Tower had to have heard what I'd done last night, and I had no doubt by tomorrow morning, if not sooner, everyone would have heard that one tap from Lord Rider made me collapse in pain.

The guys had asked me how training went, and I'd given the briefest replies as possible while wolfing down my meal, determined to get away from all the prying eyes as fast as I could. I had to get back to— hell, get *started with* being unnoticed and to do that I needed to stop drawing attention to myself.

The other novices had already shown that they wanted to put me in my place and the sooner it looked like I was there, the better. And it certainly didn't help that I'd drawn the attention of the Captain of the Gold Tower.

I couldn't let the others think Talon was giving me special treatment. That would only increase their desire to remind me that I wasn't a noble anymore, that I was no longer anyone special. And while my body wanted special treatment from him, Lord Quill and — shadows! — even Lord Rider, the rest of me really really didn't.

I was now almost done with my half shift in the stables and my body *still* throbbed with the need Talon had inspired just by looking at me.

That moment just outside the pasture gate had been breathtaking and consuming, filling me with such yearning that it had taken everything I'd had to resist his command and take my shirt off.

Great Father I *still* wanted to take off my shirt and all my other clothes as well. And while a part of me was relieved I hadn't, another part was shaken at how close I'd come to ruining everything on my first day. And an even larger part of me couldn't stop thinking about Talon's gorgeous body, the last trickles of water trailing over his sculpted muscles and his large—

What would it feel like to have him pushing into me? To have his swirling, mesmerizing gaze capturing mine and him fulfilling the promise inspired by his magic?

It didn't seem to matter that my whole body hurt from a full day of physical labor. The achy part low within me that had awakened last night when that man had put his mouth on me throbbed with a need I feared I wasn't going to be able to satisfy. Especially since I was sure going to the Garden had been a mistake. And now that the burn of the magic binding me to the Black Tower was gone, I was never going there again.

I gritted my teeth and ran the large grooming brush down the side of the dappled gray mare in front of me. She eyed me but continued to stay calm, unlike some of the other horses the other stable hand had been assigned to groom, and I was grateful Kasen, the stablemaster, had taken pity on me and given me the most docile animals in the stable.

"Times up," a cheery voice said, and the man whose shift I'd been given — what was his name? Right. Vyell — strode up to the stable door with a big grin brightening his face. Except I was pretty sure the grin was for the horse and not me, since so far only a small handful of Guardsmen had been happy to see me today.

"How's he treating you, sweetheart?" he asked as he stepped inside, and ran a hand over the horse's flank. "She looks good."

"She better," Kasen said from his spot a few stalls down. "He spent double the amount of time he should have on her and the other nine horses he's groom so far."

"Yeah, but his arms are so short, he probably has to do double the brush strokes to get the job done," Vyell called back with a chuckle.

Kasen huffed a gruff laugh. "You better have groomed fifteen by the time your shift ends tomorrow, Sawyer, or I'll hold you back to finish your work. Now be gone with you."

I handed Vyell the brush and hurried out of the stables before Kasen could change his mind. I'd been slow because I didn't have a lot of experience grooming horses and because my whole body hurt... and because I was still thoroughly distracted by Talon and his magic.

At the thought of his name, a shiver of need rushed through me. If I was smart, I'd avoid him from now on.

With what his magic did to me, it was only a matter of time before I was no longer able to resist, and he'd learn the truth. That couldn't happen for at least a month, longer if I was really lucky, since Sawyer needed at minimum a month to get out of the Five Great Kingdoms. Except how could I avoid him without looking like I was avoiding him? Because being obvious would just raise his suspicions as well.

Maybe I could tell him his magic made me uncomfortable. Not to mention the fact that he'd used his magical influence to try to get me to undress and now I *was* a little afraid of him.

That was probably the best plan to get him to stay away from me, but something inside me twisted tight at that idea. I had so few allies here, and if I alienated Talon, would I also alienate Kit, Payne, and Lewin?

I didn't know how friendly they were with him since he hadn't taken the midday or evening meal with them like he had with the morning meal, but pushing Talon away risked pushing them away and, as much as I should, I didn't want to go through my time here completely alone.

Except that was the best option. Head down. No friends. Do what needed to be done and keep my secret for as long as possible.

I dragged myself up the three flights of stairs and down the halls to my room. Making friends would only make keeping my secret more difficult, but I had a suspicion that Kit and Payne wouldn't let me ignore them during mealtime. I was already trapped with an association to them and at least they didn't care that I'd screwed up and endangered lives.

Which still left the problem with Talon and my sore, throbbing body.

Shadows, I was so tired, and I wasn't looking forward to another morning of shoveling shit or being tripped on the running trail.

I entered my room, making sure the latch had caught on my door, then took off my vambraces and jerkin before unlacing the ties on my shirt and pulling it off. The strips of cloth flattening my breasts were a little loose, but still tight enough to hide my figure even after an afternoon of running and fighting and grooming. The bruise running up my side and over my chest was an ugly dark purple and had grown bigger since I'd woken this morning.

It was no surprise both Talon and Lord Quill had looked shocked when I'd showed it to them, and I'd known the moment Talon had told Lord Quill to take a look that I'd had to at least give them a peek. I was just grateful bringing up Edred's bad temper had been enough of a distraction that they hadn't demanded to see all of it.

Although it had been a huge surprise that Lord Quill then wanted to go and rescue me.

Had he felt the same strange compulsion I had when we'd first met? I'd thought I'd been unable to stop looking at him because I'd never seen a fae before or because he had a magic that compelled someone to look at him.

But now I'd experienced real compelling magic and that hadn't been what I'd experienced with Lord Quill. It had been softer, warmer, a call to something deep within me that made my pulse flutter.

As it was, I could only hope Lord Quill accepted my

explanation and wouldn't want proof that I was safe. That, and while it hadn't been the whole truth, it made for a good excuse as to why I'd been stupid enough to use the ring after dark. Maybe word would get out that I'd done it in defense of family and the men would go back to thinking I was an insignificant runt not worth their notice.

I could only hope.

I finished getting undressed, put the plug in the basin and filled it halfway. Using just the basin wasn't going to be the easiest or fastest way to clean myself, but it beat using the baths in the middle of the night and hoping no one stumbled across me. I worked the sweet-smelling soap I'd taken from the towel room into a lather and scrubbed at the grime on my hands, making sure the scrapes I'd gotten from my fall on the running trail were thoroughly cleaned.

Exhaustion pulled at me, the world turning soft and dim, and my thoughts stuttered. I'd been turning the soap around and around in my hands and not moving into the next step of washing the rest of myself.

Jeez. I had no idea how I was going to manage more mornings in the stables or afternoons of running and sparring. One day and I was ready to collapse. How was I going to manage a whole rotation of it or more?

Darkness fluttered across my vision.

If I didn't hurry up, I was going to pass out half

washed. Good thing the room was so small it'd be easy to make it to my bed before I collapsed.

I dunked one of my small towels into the water, worked the lather into it, and ran it up my arm, trying to pick up my pace, but the darkness swelled, suddenly overwhelming me and a sense of fear and urgency surged inside me.

My pulse tripped. Another premonition? But I'd had two yesterday. I'd had as many premonitions in the last two days as I'd had all last year.

A thick, cold mist rushed around my legs and swept over the basin, and my muscles started to tremble. I tried to reach for the basin to catch my balance but missed and fell to my knees. Then a frozen gust of wind tore the mist away, revealing the Gray's ragged barren landscape and the towering Shadow Gate off in the distance.

The basin was gone and so too was the wall to my room. In front of me lay a body with a shock of red hair dressed in the black uniform of a Guardsman. He lay facing away from me, but I knew the body could only be Sawyer's. While there could be someone else in the Tower with the same red hair, I doubted my premonition— no my *vision* would show me a stranger. Not with the same soul-crushing fear that had overwhelmed me the first time I'd been shown Sawyer's lifeless body in the Gray.

But seeing it now meant I hadn't changed the

future, that I was going to be discovered and they were going to find Sawyer and drag him to the Black Tower, something I couldn't let happen.

Except I didn't know how to stop it. I'd been thinking about how to deal with Talon and the others a moment ago. Did that mean I was making a mistake by not forcing them away? Or would forcing them away make this vision happen faster.

A pair of brown boots stepped into sight and the mist parted, revealing just enough of a man so I could tell he wasn't a Guardsman but not actually see who it was. He chuckled, the sound dark, twisting my fear tighter, and he kicked Sawyer's body, rolling him over and making the mist billow around him like a thick blanket, obscuring him completely.

"Leave him for the shadows," someone in the mist behind the man said.

"Yeah," he replied, his voice a harsh whisper, and he marched away, making the mist whirl with the movement and slide away from Sawyer's body.

Except it wasn't Sawyer's body.

It was mine.

My fear snapped into a desperate panic that crushed around my heart and stole my breath. My face was a ruined mess, swelling from what had to have been multiple blows, my nose was broken and bleeding, and I'd left a large puddle of blood on the ground, while another was forming around my head as I watched. I'd been stabbed at least once, but with my black clothing and the swirling mist, I couldn't see where.

I tried to look around to see if there was anyone who'd help me, but the mist surged then bled into darkness, and my premonition spat me back into my room in the Black Tower.

Shadows! I *had* changed the future. Now *I* was the one who was going to die in front of the Shadow Gate.

Don't miss the next book in the series!

Stand Against the Rising Storm
Desperate Disguise: Book Two

A terrifying vision of a deadly future...

I've risked everything to save my brother and taken his place in the Black Guard, and now my vision of his death has changed. I'm the one who'll be murdered.

I don't know when it will happen, but I'm magically bound to the Black Tower and can't leave. I also can't turn myself in until my brother escapes the kingdom or my sacrifice will be for nothing... because once everyone knows I'm a woman, I'll be punished and imprisoned.

My only hope is to survive the Guard's grueling training and pray I'm strong enough to change my future.

But that isn't easy. The other guardsmen are bigger and stronger than me and are determined to put me in my place, I have a growing attraction to the beautiful fae leaders of the Black Guard: the enigmatic Lord Commander Rider, the charming Lord Quill, and the alluring Talon.

To complicate matters further, I find myself inexplicably drawn to the fae garden each night, where a mysterious Fantasy Man awakens a passion I never knew existed.

Time is running out, and the stakes have never been higher. I must keep my identity a secret and become a warrior... because I've seen what happens if I fail.

Other Books by Tessa Cole

Wolf Deceived, book 1

Wolf Denied, book 2

Wolf Desired, book 3

Wolf Distressed, book 4

Wolf Decided, book 5

Wolf Devoted, book 6

THE GRECIAN GODDESS TRILOGY

Written with Clara Wils

Kiss of the Goddess, book 1

Power of the Goddess, book 2

Bonds of the Goddess, book 3

SECRETS GODS KEEP

Written with Clara Wils

Craving Demons, book 1

Chaos Demons, book 2

Claiming Demons, book 3

HER BAD BOY WOLVES

Written with Clara Wils

Pack Against the Wall, book 1

Want you Pack, book 2

Pack in Business, book 3